The kitchen window shattered with a pop.

"Get down!" Aiden was already in motion as the words left his mouth.

At the same time, Charlie drew her 9mm, taking a defensive stance.

More bullets buzzed through the air and punched holes in the cabinets, sending jagged plywood shards in all directions.

They had one big problem. The rifle trained on them.

Charlie? Her name was on his tongue when she came crawling around the kitchen island with her STI Staccato-P, locked and loaded, in hand.

Another volley of gunfire tore through the room.

Distance. Aiden needed distance from the scene.

Impossibly rapid gunfire w̶̶ ̶̶ntrolled, calculated. Bullets whizzed way too̶ ̶̶ ̶̶ ̶̶'̶̶s comfort. The shooter's accuracy ̶̶ ̶̶ ̶̶ ̶̶ ̶̶ ̶̶ ̶̶ was well trained, statio̶̶ ̶̶ ̶̶ ̶̶ ̶̶ ̶̶ spot-on, idea of where̶̶ ̶̶ ̶̶ ̶̶ ̶̶ ̶̶ ̶̶ blinds and the fact tha̶̶ ̶̶ ̶̶ ̶̶ ̶̶ ̶̶ apparently weren't conceale̶̶ ̶̶ ̶̶ ̶̶ explanation.

Their sniper had a precision-guided smart scope that could track targets behind walls.

WITNESS SECURITY BREACH

JUNO RUSHDAN

HARLEQUIN
INTRIGUE

For those who fear love.

ISBN-13: 978-1-335-13679-4

Recycling programs for this product may not exist in your area.

Witness Security Breach

Copyright © 2020 by Juno Rushdan

This edition published by arrangement with Harlequin Books S.A.

For questions and comments about the quality of this book, please contact us at CustomerService@Harlequin.com.

Harlequin Enterprises ULC
22 Adelaide St. West, 40th Floor
Toronto, Ontario M5H 4E3, Canada
www.Harlequin.com

Printed in U.S.A.

Juno Rushdan is the award-winning author of steamy, action-packed romantic thrillers that keep you on the edge of your seat. She writes about kick-ass heroes and strong heroines fighting for their lives as well as their happily-ever-afters. As a veteran air force intelligence officer, she uses her background supporting special forces to craft realistic stories that make you sweat and swoon. Juno currently lives in the DC area with her patient husband, two rambunctious kids and a spoiled rescue dog. To receive a FREE book from Juno, sign up for her newsletter at junorushdan.com/mailing-list. Also be sure to follow Juno on BookBub for the latest on sales at bit.ly/BookBubjuno.

Books by Juno Rushdan

Harlequin Intrigue

A Hard Core Justice Thriller

Hostile Pursuit
Witness Security Breach

Visit the Author Profile page at Harlequin.com.

CAST OF CHARACTERS

Aiden Yazzie—He's the best in the Special Operations Group (SOG)—highly trained tactical US marshals brought in when extraordinary measures are necessary. He's been in love with his partner for years, but he doesn't want a fling with her. Only forever is enough.

Charlotte "Charlie" Killinger—A hard-charging former marine and one of the few women in the elite ranks of the SOG. Her complicated past has left a hole in her heart that she's tried to fill with her job. She keeps everyone at a distance, even her partner and best friend, Aiden.

Eugene Potter/Edgar Plinski—This witness hasn't told the Department of Justice all that he knows for a reason and his secret endangers everyone around him.

Nick McKenna—A good friend of Aiden, Charlie's ex-lover and a colleague.

William "Big Bill" Walsh—Self-made and uncompromising, he's a mob boss with a vendetta and won't let anyone take what's his without a fight.

Frank Devlin—A ruthless mercenary on Walsh's payroll.

Ava Garcia—FBI agent building a case against William Walsh.

Chapter One

The next four words to leave his mouth would obliterate a life. Four words every US marshal hated saying. Four words every person in the witness security program dreaded hearing.

"You're in imminent danger," Aiden Yazzie said, closing the last set of kitchen blinds, muting the bright April sun. He turned and met Eugene Potter's terrified face.

The urgency of the situation was spelled out in big, bold letters across the bulletproof vests of Aiden's four-man special operations team, the CAR-15 rifles strapped across their backs and the tactical, turbocharged vehicle with blacked-out windows parked in front of the suburban Palisades home. When the US Marshals Service identified a need for extraordinary measures, it was the Special Operations Group—SOG—that answered the call.

The sixty-two-year-old man staggered back and sat on a stool at the counter. "But how?" He ran a shaking hand through his thinning gray hair. "I've been so careful. How was I blown?"

Aiden exchanged a glance with his partner and best friend, Charlotte "Charlie" Killinger. The answer to Eugene's question had the entire Justice Department in an uproar, had tarnished the impeccable reputation of their San Diego field office and sent the SOG scrambling.

Eugene had a right to know, along with the other unsuspecting individuals in the program that'd been compromised in the Pacific Coast region, but the reason was classified.

In typical Killinger fashion, Charlie redirected. "If you want to live, we have to relocate you again. Immediately."

"I—I can't." Eugene's mouth hung open, and his eyes blinked rapidly. "My wife is at work."

Aiden stepped up beside the trembling man. "We're prepared to pick her up before we head to the Safe Site and Protection Center. At the SSPC, you'll both be briefed." He put a hand on the older man's shoulder. Tension coursed through Aiden. Each minute they spent in the house endangered Potter. "We should leave now."

"You don't understand." Eugene shook his head. "We've only been married six months. I followed procedure. Sharon doesn't know who I really am or the things I've done." Despite the air-conditioning that matched the temperate SoCal weather, a sweat broke out on his brow. Propping an elbow on the counter, he wiped his forehead with the heel of his palm.

"It's good you followed protocol. Smart," Charlie said in a clipped tone, flicking a look at her watch. "I'll explain why you couldn't have disclosed the details."

Those in WITSEC left everything behind, buried the old version of themselves and were instructed never to share the truth or their past with anyone. Not even a new spouse.

In the event of an ugly divorce, the secret could be divulged out of revenge.

Starting a marriage based on lies was brutal. But not as brutal as a bullet to the head.

Following the rules kept people alive and no witness who'd done so had ever been killed. It was Aiden and Charlie's job to make sure that didn't change.

"She'll know I lied to her!" Eugene's face snapped up. "She'll question everything. My love. Our marriage." His gaze flew to the photo gallery above the breakfast nook. Family memories featuring young children adorned the wall. "Sharon will never leave San Diego. Her four kids are here, six grandbabies. Cindy, her youngest, is pregnant with her first. I thought I'd be here for the rest of my life. It's the reason I married her, allowed myself to become part of the family. You people promised that after I testified and got settled, I'd be fine." His features twisted in pain, his eyes brimming with tears. "I'm going to be sick." He jumped to his feet and ran into the hallway bathroom, shutting the door behind him.

"What's taking so long?" Johnny Torres asked over the comms device in their ears.

He and Dale Banks were the other two tactical marshals assigned to the high-priority detail. They were covering the front and rear of the house.

"The *dynamic duo* should've had this wrapped up by now," Dale said, his tone caustic.

Aiden rolled his eyes. He and Charlie were indeed dynamic together. They were the best SOG operators in the unit. Smack talk came with the territory. Under normal circumstances he would've enjoyed it, but after taking a wrecking ball to a man's life, he wasn't in the mood.

Charlie met his gaze. Those sapphire-blue eyes of hers were hard as gemstones. Held an incisive gleam that never dulled. With blond hair cut in a sleek bob, her fair skin and icy veneer, she was stunningly good-looking, and called the snow queen by the other guys.

To Aiden, she was more of a Viking warrior ready for battle. She was simply spectacular.

She toggled her earpiece. "If we want your opinions, we'll give it to you. Torres, start the car. We're leaving the wife behind and heading straight to the SSPC." She disconnected.

After Torres gave a curt acknowledgment over comms, Aiden asked her, "Isn't that premature? Mr. Potter might want to try to convince his wife to go with him."

"Did you take a gander at that?" Charlie hooked her thumbs in her gun belt and inclined her head toward the picture-perfect wall of photos. "Each person is an anchor, weighting his new bride to her old life. He never should've been foolish enough to fall in love and buy into some fairy-tale ending. A clean break is best."

"It takes courage to love." Aiden strode up to her, bringing them face-to-face. Their eyes locked. "Don't knock it until you're brave enough to try it."

Charlie slinked closer, sexy as sin, and hoisted her chin like a gladiator, quickening his pulse. They would've been nose to nose if he didn't have a good six inches on her.

"What you call bravery, I see as delusion." Her voice was low and cold but heated his skin.

For a second, he was tempted to lower his head and kiss her. Melt her glacial facade with all the red-hot passion burning in his veins that wasn't professional or platonic, but restraint bred from lots and lots of practice had become one of his virtues.

When he made his move, it had to be the right time and place. He didn't want to be one of Charlie's lovers who had the shelf life of bread. He wanted to be the love of her life.

"Leaving Mrs. Potter behind with a clean break isn't our decision to make," he said.

"Nevertheless, Tweedledee and Tweedledum outside have a point. This is taking too long. We agreed that we'd be in and out in ten minutes."

Aiden didn't need to check his watch to instinctively know they'd been inside for six. Already his gut agreed with Charlie. They'd been there too long.

"You still have that bad feeling?" she asked, her hand resting on the gun on her hip.

The moment they'd pulled up, it was as if a clammy finger had been dragged down his spine.

He wished he could chalk it up to nerves over keeping his big news from Charlie. Telling her that this might be their last assignment together if he accepted the coveted position as an SOG instructor at Camp Beauregard in Louisiana. It was a conversation he wanted to have about as much as he wanted to get a root canal without Novocain. But *this* wasn't nerves.

Aiden stepped away, scrubbing a palm over his jaw. "Yeah, I still have it."

"You might be in denial about your sixth sense, but I'm not. I've learned the hard way never to ignore your gift."

Denial couldn't be further from the truth. If experience was any indication, the prickly tingle warned that someone was going to die today.

Was it a *gift* to know when death was going to come calling? Felt more like a curse.

"We can't wait for Eugene to pull it together." Charlie shifted her weight from one foot to the other. Crossed her arms over her chest. "We need to go."

No bad feeling necessary to realize that was an understatement.

There was a high price on Eugene's head. His personal information had been sold on the dark web. At least one hit man that they were aware of had been contracted, prompting the urgent relocation. It was possible others might come slithering out of the gutter to try to collect.

A toilet flushed and water ran.

Eugene stumbled out of the bathroom, looking peaked and more devastated than before. "I need to talk to Sharon, say goodbye at the very least. Tell her I'm sorry. I owe her that."

Aiden threw Charlie an I-told-you-so look, which she returned with a conciliatory nod.

"Let me grab something first," Eugene said, "and then we can go."

"There's no time for you to pack anything." Aiden sidestepped, blocking his path. "All the essentials will be at the SSPC, just like last time."

"It'll only take a second. I won't leave without it." Eugene pivoted, scurrying around him to the open shelving beside the stove, which was lined with cookbooks, dishes and knickknacks. He took down a display of wine corks in a tall glass vase, dumped them onto the counter and fished out one from the pile. A relieved look washed over him. "Okay. Now we can g—"

The kitchen window shattered with a pop.

"Get down!" Aiden was already in motion as the words left his mouth.

He lunged for Eugene. At the same time, Charlie drew her 9 mm, taking a defensive posture.

Aiden shoved Eugene hard to the floor as the vase on the counter shattered, spraying glass over them. More bullets buzzed through the air and punched holes in the cabinets, sending jagged plywood shards in all directions.

They had one big problem. The rifle trained on them.

Covering his head with his hands, Eugene shrieked but had the sense to stay pinned in the chaos of the fusillade.

Aiden tightened his hold on him, ensuring Eugene was shielded. No bullet would reach Eugene unless it went through Aiden first.

Charlie? Her name was on his tongue when she came crawling around the kitchen island with her STI Staccato-P, locked and loaded, in hand. Only SOG carried the STI rather than the Glock 22 that rank-and-file marshals were issued. What elite operator didn't want a gun that held twenty-one rounds, shot superfast and never failed in accuracy?

Another volley of gunfire tore through the room.

Distance. Aiden needed distance from the scene.

He pushed back mentally, slowed down the external factors along with his breathing and the rush of blood through his ears. His soul quieted.

His mind brought everything into razor-sharp focus, discarding every distraction in seconds.

From the sound, the rifle being used was suppressed. Based on the I-want-to-blow-off-your-head-sized holes in the cupboards, it was also high-powered.

The impossibly rapid gunfire was controlled, calculated. Bullets whizzed way too close for Aiden's comfort. The shooter's accuracy indicated that he or she was well trained, stationary, and had a good, if not spot-on, idea of where they were despite the drawn blinds. Aiden had got Eugene behind cover—but apparently they weren't concealed. Which left only one explanation.

Their sniper had a precision-guided smart scope that could track targets behind walls. "Shooter is using LIDAR or ultrasonic technology," Aiden said to Charlie.

"Must be military grade."

If they didn't want to ingest lead, sitting there wasn't an option.

"We've got to move," Aiden said. "Now!" Not waiting for Eugene to react, he grabbed the older man by the collar and hauled him up to his knees.

Bullets peppered the spot where they'd been.

They shuffled forward. Aiden used his own body as cover. Glass crunched beneath them.

A maelstrom of rounds strafed the kitchen all around, riddling the drywall with holes. A hot slug sliced past their heads.

Too close. One centimeter closer and Aiden would've been toast.

Eugene fumbled, a panicked flush on his cheeks. The wine cork slipped from his grasp.

"I need it!" He had the reckless gall to resist moving and reached back for the cork. A piece of glass sliced open his palm, drawing blood.

Eugene yelped from the small cut like he'd been shot.

Aiden pushed him lower and grabbed the wine cork. Rather than handing it over, he held on to it and forced Eugene toward the refrigerator.

The fridge was one of those massive units, a sixty-four-inch side-by-side fridge-and-freezer set.

Aiden opened the fridge and tucked Eugene behind the door.

"Give it to me!" Eugene tried to wrest the cork from Aiden's hand.

If he was more concerned with a piece of bark than taking a bullet, no way in hell was Aiden giving it to him.

Eugene snatched hold of one end of the wine cork and pulled on it, separating it in half, revealing a concealed flash drive.

"What is this?" Aiden asked, holding tight to the drive.

"I need it!" Eugene clawed at Aiden's fingers like his life depended on getting it back.

Aiden shoved him against the interior of the fridge before he waved Charlie over to take the other side. There was only space for two behind the doors.

"Torres, Banks," Charlie said over comms, her voice like steel as she made her way to the refrigerator, "we're taking gunfire. What's your status?"

"I left the vehicle. I'm headed inside to help get Potter out," Torres responded.

Any assassin worth his weight in salt would have both exits covered. Taking Eugene outside would only increase his exposure. They'd never get him to the car alive.

Aiden tapped his earpiece. "Torres, don't. Track where the gunfire is coming from and lay down suppressive fire to give me a chance to move. We've got to kill the sniper first."

"On it."

"Banks?" Aiden waited for the next reply that didn't come. "Dale, come in."

"I think he's down," Charlie said, echoing his thoughts.

If that were the case, the sniper did have a line of sight to the backyard, kitchen, most likely the front, too, and had taken out Banks before unleashing a torrent of slugs on them.

"Protect Potter," Aiden said to Charlie. "The fridge door will make better cover and take the brunt of the gunfire."

He guessed the rifle was a .50 cal. The thick stainless-steel doors wouldn't hold up indefinitely under the heavy firepower, but they should withstand the onslaught long enough for Aiden to take care of the shooter.

"You stay," Charlie said, her eyes bright and shining, her voice too eager. "I'll go—"

"No. It's an order." Aiden only played the I-outrank-you card when necessary. It wasn't that Charlie couldn't handle the sniper—she was more than capable, but she was drawn to danger like a moth to a flame, and he'd do anything to prevent her from getting burned.

Coming up on one knee, he drew his gun and then moved without hesitation toward the door leading to the yard. He'd be easy pickings once outside. Since Banks had taken the back, Aiden didn't know if there was anything out there that he could use for cover besides a couple of stone pillars.

A grill. He recalled noticing a gas grill on the patio as he'd lowered the blinds, but the propane tank made it more of a hazard than potential cover.

Going outside was a dicey move, but necessary. Eliminating the threat required two people. One as bait to draw fire while the other went in and neutralized the enemy.

Aiden stopped before reaching the doors and stood with his back to the double-wall ovens in a pocket of space protected from gunfire. "Torres, you got a bead on our sniper?" Aiden asked, slipping the thumb drive into his pocket.

"Yep. He's on the roof of the house on the west side."

The location made perfect sense based on the lines of sight, and would put the sun at the shooter's back, but the gunman hadn't been out in the open when they'd arrived at the exact same time Eugene had been pulling into the driveway, returning from errands. The sniper must've set up while Aiden and Charlie had been indoors explaining things to Eugene. Risked pulling off the hit in broad daylight rather than taking the chance of losing his target.

"I need a distraction so I can move," Aiden said.

"Got it. Be ready on my mark."

Aiden glanced at Charlie.

The fridge doors were doing a good job of absorbing the bullets. Charlie would make sure Potter didn't lose his head, literally or figuratively.

Aiden braced for what was to come, for what he had to do next.

An icy stillness stole over him. His heart pounded, but he grew utterly calm. Resolved. Focused on nothing except the plan forming with brutal clarity. Warfare meditation.

"Go now," Torres said in his ear.

Gunshots from a handgun rang out. As expected, the suppressed rifle fire refocused.

Aiden dashed through the dining area, slipped outside and shut the door.

In the grass, Dale Banks was down on his back. Blood pooled from a hole in what was left of his head. Aiden's gut clenched at the thought of Dale's pregnant wife and how there wouldn't be an open casket.

Aiden pressed his spine hard against a stone column, ensuring he wasn't in the line of fire. Then he drew on honed professional detachment.

Low pops from the big rifle whizzed in the direction where Torres must've taken position on the side of Potter's house.

This was Aiden's chance. It wouldn't last long.

He took two deep breaths and bolted toward the fence, racing across the spacious yard before the shooter spotted him. He scaled the six-foot wooden barrier with little effort while Torres played decoy.

Making his way around the adjacent ranch-style house, Aiden crossed the short distance to the far side of the home. He had to sneak up on the sniper's rear and deal with him quickly.

A trash bin had been propped against a section of the stucco wall alongside an AC unit. The shooter must've used it to get up to the second floor, where there was a broken window.

No time to go through the house to get to the roof. Besides, the plastic receptacle might make unwanted noise or buckle under his weight, giving him away.

He searched for a better option.

Fragrant honeysuckle climbed a trellis that screened either side of the back porch.

The wooden lattice might be perfect. Provided it was sturdy enough.

A quick shake after putting his full weight on two bottom rungs showed it to be a durable frame that'd been built to last.

Aiden holstered his firearm and scaled the privacy trellis. He climbed smoothly, moving from one hand-hold to another. At the top, he hoisted himself up onto the patio roof and landed softly, straining not to make a sound.

The sniper was clad in all black and in a prone position only several feet away, cheek pressed against the stock, trying to put holes in Torres.

Aiden crept forward. Slipped his sidearm from the holster on his hip. "Freeze! Or I'll blow your head off."

The semiautomatic gunfire stopped. The shooter stilled.

"Hands up off the rifle. Now!" Aiden stepped closer, aiming for the shoulder. If he had to shoot, he'd prefer to wound him so they could question him and find out exactly who'd taken out the contract on Eugene.

Slowly, the man with a buzz cut complied, raising his gloved hands to ear level, staying down on his belly.

Aiden unhooked handcuffs from his gun belt and tossed them over to the guy. They clattered next to his left elbow. "Cuff yourself. Hands behind your back. Take it nice and slow."

"Please, don't shoot," the sniper said with a heavy twang that came from somewhere below the Mason-Dixon line. "I'm just going for the handcuffs."

Dixie reached across his body with his right hand toward the cuffs, posture tightening, muscles shifting gradually. No sudden moves. Fingers dipped out of sight in front of his chest.

Then a lot of things happened in a flash.

The killer rotated lightning quick, flipping onto his back.

In the same heartbeat, Aiden squeezed the trigger. Missed by a hair and hit a roof shingle because the assassin had been anticipating it, prepared for it.

Steel glinted in the sun. Fast, so fast, Aiden almost didn't see the fracture of light as the hit man threw a knife.

If Aiden had blinked, he would've been dead.

He ducked, narrowly avoiding a tactical blade to the throat. But the gunman launched himself up to his feet while throwing a second knife in one smooth motion.

The four-inch combat knife struck Aiden in the bicep, destabilizing his firing arm.

Dixie rushed him, two hundred pounds of desperate muscle charging.

Aiden used the nanoseconds he had and lowered his own center of mass, grounding his body weight for the impact.

The blow was harder than expected. Aiden used momentum, sending his enemy up from the ground and overhead.

But Dixie grabbed hold of Aiden and ensured they both went down.

They tumbled. Pure kinetic energy propelled two conflicting forces. They rolled and rolled right over the edge, plummeted, falling.

Aiden threw a knee into the other man's gut and twisted, positioning himself on top.

The ground rushed up to greet them.

Dixie's head smacked against the AC unit with a nauseating crunch.

Aiden slammed down hard, his bones jarred, the breath forced from his lungs, the blade knocked from his arm, but the hit man's body had helped cushion the fall.

He rolled off the body. The contract killer's head lay at an unnatural angle, his neck snapped. That was when Aiden spotted it.

A wireless, flesh-colored comms device tucked in the dead man's ear.

The sniper wasn't alone.

Chapter Two

Dead silence.

Aiden must've stopped the sniper. Of course he had. Whenever her partner set his mind to a task, he accomplished it no matter what.

Charlie clasped Eugene's shoulder and gave him a quick once-over, making sure he wasn't injured.

Eugene let out a ragged breath he'd been holding. Other than a bloody palm, he was fine.

The kitchen looked like a war zone. The sniper had turned the cabinets into Swiss cheese and every breakable item that had been in Eugene's vicinity had been shattered.

They were lucky not to have been torn to pieces.

Charlie rose, finger on the trigger of her 9 mm, and stepped out from behind the fridge door, then stopped cold.

A prickle of alarm streaked up her nape, tightening every hair on her scalp. The back door was ajar. Aiden had closed it behind him when he left. She was certain of it.

Charlie raised her palm, urging Eugene to stay put and keep quiet. He clung tighter to a shelf inside the fridge, understanding the silent warning.

Nothing stood out. No overt sign of lingering danger caught her attention.

But that open door was wrong.

Her intuition wasn't nearly as razor-sharp as Aiden's, but her situational awareness—the instinct that flared if you were walking down a dark alley or found a door open that should've been closed—was finely tuned and had kept her alive after four years in tactical operations.

Charlie remained perfectly still and listened.

There. Not a breath. Not movement. *A presence.* Someone else in the room with them.

Then the whisper-soft slide of footsteps across the wood floor.

Her blood ran cold. She dropped to a low crouch behind the kitchen island with her gun leveled. Had the sniper taken out Torres, too, evaded Aiden and got into the house?

The prospect of Aiden being hurt or worse was unconscionable.

Another subtle scrape across the hardwood. Glass crunched underfoot and it wasn't hers.

"Charlie," Aiden said in a ragged groan over comms in her ear. "The sniper isn't alone."

His little news flash was thirty seconds late. Aiden's timing sucked, but she breathed an inward sigh of relief that he was alive. *Thank God.*

"Charlie? Are you all right?" Aiden's usual smooth, carefree voice sounded rough-edged, more than winded. He must've been really hurting. "Come in."

Responding or calling for backup would've only given away her exact position. That was the absolute worst thing she could do.

Shifting the angle of her body, she peered through the holes of the cabinets.

Movement on the other side of the island. A shuffle. Rustle of debris.

Pressure already on the trigger of her gun, as soon as she glimpsed a shadow, Charlie squeezed, sending a bullet into the silhouette.

With an audible grunt, the person changed course. Charlie adjusted likewise.

Instead of tracking the shadow as training had taught her, getting sucked into a game of cat and mouse while uncertain who was higher on the food chain, she did the unexpected. She leaped up and slid across the countertop to the other side of the island, landing at the back of a man shrouded in black.

She was about to fire, but he pivoted and threw a leg sweep, moving with a speed and grace that defied his great bulk. The maneuver caught her behind the Achilles, launching her feet out from under her.

Charlie's primary weapon left her grasp and went skittering across the floor as she hit the hardwood flat on her back. Landed right on top of her CAR-15 and secondary firearm that was lodged against her spinal column.

Agony exploded through her lumbar and skull. Scorching pain spasmed in every nerve along her spine. She gasped for air and swallowed the scream rising in her throat.

Through watering eyes, she spied the hit man's injury.

Charlie had shot the thick, wide bruiser in the side.

Dark red blood seeped between his gloved fingers where he applied pressure to the wound.

She fought through the haze of pain and kicked him in the gut, using both feet and all her might.

He doubled over, pressing harder to his injured side. His face stretched wide in a grimace. The tattoo on his neck of an alligator's head with a skull in its open mouth looked like it was melting.

This guy was big, skilled enough to get close without her knowing, had a high tolerance for pain since he was still standing, and was *armed*.

The gun locked in his hand was the biggest immediate threat.

Charlie threw a boot heel to his groin, redirecting his focus away from aiming and putting a bullet in her head. Another precise kick to his knee, over and over, until she heard the sharp, cracking noise of the kneecap shattering. A howl of anguish tore from his lips.

A well-aimed kick was a woman's ultimate defense.

She didn't stop there and rammed the heel of her foot up into his face, crushing his nose.

He stumbled backward, his arms windmilling in a hopeless struggle for balance that he'd never regain. Blood gushed from his nostrils.

Seizing the momentary advantage, she rolled onto her side, pulled her backup Glock 27 subcompact from the holster at the small of her back, aimed center mass and blew a hole in her attacker.

The force of the bullet wasn't enough to knock the big guy down. He stood motionless, hovering in animated death for an instant, and then tipped forward face-first.

Charlie rolled out of the way.

He hit the floor with a nauseating thud. She looked at his face, stared in his vacant eyes.

She'd killed a man. He'd been trying to kill her and a witness. Extensive training had fortified her for this, but nothing truly prepared her for the stark reality.

Next thing she knew, Torres came in hot through the front, making a beeline for Potter.

Aiden hustled inside through the back door, coming to her side. "Are you all right?" he asked, his proximity sending a rush of warmth through her. He proffered a hand.

Charlie accepted the assistance up and onto her feet, shaking off the vestiges of pain. She took in Aiden's mussed black hair and his deep brown eyes. He looked uncharacteristically weary, and his softer brown complexion that spoke of his Native American heritage was pallid. A nick marred his cheek, but there was a nastier gash on his arm.

Her breath hitched, her chest tightening. "You're hurt."

The deep cut was below the sleeve of his tight black T-shirt. Blood ran in rivulets down his muscular arm and dripped from his fingers.

This was the first time he'd ever been injured on the job in six years and she'd borne witness during the past four that they'd been partners. Not so much as a scratch.

An impressive SOG record that made him a figure of near-mythic proportion in their elite ranks.

"We've got to stop the bleeding, bandage it." She hated the sound of fear that leaked into her voice. Pushing hair behind her ear, she summoned her composure. "You might need stitches."

"It has to wait," Aiden said. "I'll bandage it in the car and worry about stitches after we get to the SSPC."

Always self-sacrificing. Always a pillar of strength. Always so darn hard to resist.

Aiden crouched next to the dead body and reached for something she'd completely missed. A black nylon belt bag on the dead man's waist.

"What about the sniper?" Charlie asked.

Aiden unzipped the utility pouch and dumped the contents. Two loaded magazines and a cell phone fell out. He picked up the mobile device. "We took a tumble off the roof. He hit an AC unit. Neck snapped."

Tumble? She tamped down the watery, sick feeling welling up inside and retrieved her STI Staccato-P from the floor. "Let's go."

The sooner they got Aiden's wound to stop bleeding and Potter out of danger the better.

Torres took point and led the way out through the front.

Charlie and Aiden waited for Torres to give the all clear and start the SUV before they brought Eugene outside and ushered him quickly toward the vehicle.

A few neighbors gawked at them through their windows as they made their way to the curb.

She put a hand on top of Eugene's head, ensuring he didn't bump it on the frame, and helped him scramble into the third row. After putting the seat back in place, Charlie hopped into the second row.

Aiden grabbed the medical kit from one of their bags stuffed with gear. As soon as he sat beside her, Torres thrust the SUV into gear and sped off, tires screeching.

"Oh my God. Oh my God." Eugene crouched low into a ball on the seat, his teeth chattering between his words. "Do you know how close I came to getting my head blown off? I almost died."

But he hadn't. He was alive and well.

Unlike Dale Banks, whose eight-month-pregnant wife was going to have to bury him.

And Aiden had got injured in the process of protecting Eugene.

Charlie snatched the medical kit from Aiden. No way was she going to let him treat himself. Not when she was there to help. She took out gauze and pressed it to the wound. He gave a small wince and quickly washed the expression from his face.

Risking one's life was part of the job that she had got used to quickly, but one thing rubbed her wrong and she'd never get used to it. Ninety-five percent of witnesses in the program were like Eugene—not innocent bystanders but rather criminals looking to be absolved of their illegal actions and to save their own neck. Snitches who were angry, bitter and had a sense of entitlement. Like the government owed them more.

Few had the common courtesy to even say thank-you.

"Where's my Jumpdrive?" Eugene sat up. Then he looked over his shoulder and ducked back down as if at any moment the bulletproof window might explode. "You got it, didn't you?"

No *thank you*. Only entitlement. Charlie shook her head in disgust.

"As a matter of fact, I did. What is this?" Aiden asked, holding up the drive.

"My insurance policy," Eugene said.

Was he holding on to evidence he'd never turned over to the US attorney's office?

"What's on it?" Charlie inspected Aiden's wound. His cut was still bleeding in earnest and not slow-ing down fast enough. Charlie wasn't very good with blood and there was a surprising amount of it, not to mention the sharp metallic scent, but she could handle it. For Aiden. She pressed down, trying not to hurt him, and watched as he looked through the hit man's phone. It wasn't password protected.

Aiden's profile was strong and all male, given his chiseled bone structure and sensual mouth. His hair was the richest shade of black and he had long lashes most women would envy. Damn, he was gorgeous. More beautiful than any man had a right to be.

"I told you what's on it," Eugene said. "Give the drive back to me. It's mine, damn it. I need it."

"No, you didn't tell us." Aiden frowned at something on the phone. "I want details. Right now. Did you know that you can be kicked out of the program for withholding evidence? It's called obstruction of justice."

"Protecting myself isn't the same as obstructing justice." Eugene started to straighten in his seat but seemed to think better of it. "You don't have the right to confiscate my personal property."

"What property?" Charlie asked. "I don't have the faintest idea what you're talking about. Do you, Aiden?"

He shook his head. "Nope."

"You can't do this." Eugene peeked up over the seat. "Marshal, uh, you, the one driving. You can't let them do this."

"Sorry, sir. Wish I could help." Torres lifted a nonchalant hand and checked his mirrors. "But I wasn't privy to the conversation in the house. If they say they didn't take your property, then they didn't."

"Feel free to jog our memories, Eugene," Charlie

said. "Start by sharing what's on this *alleged* thumb drive."

"This is so unfair. I'm the victim in all this." Eugene sniveled until he realized there was no wiggling out of telling them. "Fine. Information on a few organizations. I kept it instead of turning it over in case I needed it someday to get out of trouble."

"Well, it seems to have gotten you into more trouble rather than saving you from it," Aiden said.

The gauze on Aiden's arm was soaked through. Charlie removed it and inspected the gash.

He looked down at the deep cut. The wound swelled with more blood and seemed as if it might never stop bleeding. He glanced up at her. "It's not that bad."

Granted, it wasn't a bullet hole. The blade had missed the brachial artery, and she didn't think the knife had struck bone, but the cut was an inch long, at least half an inch deep in muscle, and was gushing.

This was the definition of *bad*.

"I got lucky," he whispered to her as he leaned in. "Could've been my throat instead of my arm."

Her heart lurched. That was so not reassuring. At all.

"Do you know who put the hit out on you?" Aiden asked Eugene.

"Not for certain. There are mobsters in Texas, Louisiana and Mississippi who'd be happy to see me dead."

That was true. Eugene Potter was in fact Edgar Plinski, aka the Money Magician. An accountant for various organized crime outfits from Houston to Biloxi. The people he'd helped send to prison might've put the hit out on him.

Then again, it could be someone on the drive whom he still had incriminating evidence on.

"You must have some idea," Aiden pressed. "Your

life depends on this. Take a guess. Who has the biggest ax to grind with you?"

Eugene's eyes flared wide as if the answer had dawned on him, but he shook his head. "I don't know! Instead of interrogating me, isn't it your job to calm me down? Put me at ease?"

He was hiding something, perhaps protecting someone. In her gut, Charlie was certain of it.

She took out a packet of hemostatic powder from the kit and poured the brown granules into the angry wound on Aiden's arm, really getting it in there good. On contact with the blood, the tiny pellets swelled, forming a soft gel to clot the cut. It'd form a quick scab that would hold until he got stitches.

After peeling open a package of self-adhesive gauze, she applied the pad. As she gave the wound a little more pressure to help the powder set faster, she caught Eugene's eye. "The only way you'll ever truly be safe is if the people on this drive are behind bars."

Eugene, or rather Edgar, had worked for more than a handful of mobsters but had only turned state's evidence on two, claiming he didn't have anything incriminating on the others.

"The marshals at the SSPC are going to look at the contents on this drive," Aiden said. "They're going to find out whatever you're hiding. You may as well tell us, if you have any idea who might've put the hit out on you."

"It's complicated." Eugene sat up, keeping his head low. "Let's just say that someone back home had a lot invested in me. After I testified, I'm pretty sure he blew a gasket. I'm talking off the Richter scale. Okay. Satisfied? Can I have the drive now?"

"Nope," Aiden and Charlie said in unison.

"Come on," Eugene snapped.

Torres called the field office on the wireless comms to update their self-righteous, self-important leader, Will Draper, on the situation. Charlie was thankful not to hear how the loss of a good marshal was going to reflect poorly on Draper. It sure would've been nice to have a boss who cared more about his people than his career.

Inevitably, Draper would spin this, play pin-the-blame-on-someone, anyone, to keep his spotless hands clean. How on earth he'd managed to avoid the chopping block after the debacle with the breach of their WITSEC list that had occurred on his watch was anyone's guess. What happened to crap rolling uphill?

Eugene slunk down, muttering curses under his breath, protesting that he was the victim, complaining about injustice, while she finished patching up Aiden's arm and wiped blood from his skin.

The cut was deep, needed stitches and would leave a scar. Dear God, to think it could've been his throat.

Her stomach bottomed out at the idea. It took everything in Charlie not to deck ungrateful Eugene.

She poured antiseptic on a fresh piece of gauze and cleaned the cut on Aiden's face.

What would she do if she ever lost him?

Sure, they faced danger on a regular basis, and heck, the job was more fun when bullets were flying and they were kicking in doors together and slapping on handcuffs.

But today was different.

Today, hit men had got the drop on them.

Today, Aiden had fallen off a roof where *his* neck

could've been the one broken. If the contract killer's blade had found its mark—Aiden's jugular instead of his arm...

She pressed a palm to his cheek, caressed his chiseled jawline.

The intimate gesture sent an electric charge up her arm, making her nerve endings stand at attention. His expression, his piercing stare that bored straight to her soul, was just as intimate.

Perhaps more so because she knew he saw the fissures in her carefully constructed walls. When they were together, it was the only time she didn't feel alone in the world.

"I wasn't worried." She blurted out the defensive comment, having no idea where it came from.

She dropped her hand, clenching it into a fist in her lap, and forced a pretense of indifference.

Way to go, Killinger, stepping over the professional line.

But Aiden had a way of obscuring the line until she forgot it existed.

The intensity of his focus didn't waver, making the car cabin seem too small, with not enough space between them.

He covered her fist with his hand, his fingers engulfing hers. The scorching touch of his palm was hot as a brand on her skin.

"Biyooch'idi," he said. *Liar* in Navajo. The low, sensual rumble of his voice sent unbidden heat rushing to her cheeks.

She'd wanted to learn the language after going home with him, surrounded by his large family in the heart of the Navajo reservation—a sovereign territory roughly the size of West Virginia—to bury his mother. It'd been a strange trip for her, considering she no longer spoke to her own mother, but if their roles had been reversed, he would've been at her side. Aiden was eager to teach her, to share himself like turning on a faucet and letting her drink until she slaked her thirst, but Charlie was more of the sipping kind. From a disposable bottle.

What passed between them now, unspoken, reflected their bond.

One of the things she admired about Aiden was that he never called Charlie out on her BS or razzed her in front of the others, at least not in a language they understood. He'd never divulge her secrets, never betray her trust.

That was just between them, only for them—the real intimacy she treasured. And the only kind she needed. The depth of their friendship ran deeper than blood ties and she'd never do anything to jeopardize it, especially something as reckless as date him.

"Prove it." She cocked her head to the side in challenge.

"Trust me, I intend to." He gifted her with a devastating smile, flashing his annoyingly attractive dimples.

It was a punch to the gut…to her heart and, unfortunately, to her libido.

Pull yourself together. She averted her gaze and moved her hand from his, tossing the bloody gauze in a disposable motion-sickness bag.

"Did you find anything on the cell phone?" Charlie threw a glance at the device in his hand.

"Looks like a burner. With texts from only one number. Apparently, Eugene is worth two million dollars, if he's killed. An extra four million if he's brought in breathing so he can be tortured."

"Jesus, Bill," Eugene muttered low, but Charlie caught it.

He knew who was after him all right.

"That's a first," she said. "You're worth more *alive* than *dead*."

"And if any sensitive information in his possession is recovered…it's worth another four million," Aiden said.

Torres let out a low whistle. "Wow. Ten million. There's a whopper of a bull's-eye painted on your forehead," he said to Eugene. "Let's hope it's smooth sailing picking up Mrs. Potter and getting them to the SSPC."

Eugene's eyes bulged from his head as he clutched his stomach.

Charlie handed him a sick bag and turned to Aiden. "Please, tell me your *bad feeling* has gone away." Two assassins and one darn good deputy marshal were already dead. Not to mention close calls for the rest of them. That had to be the end of it. Right?

"I wish." Aiden lowered his eyes. "The feeling has only gotten worse."

Great. Why did she have to ask?

Chapter Three

William "Big Bill" Walsh was a creature of habit.

Every afternoon he sat down behind his desk to have lunch in his office at Avido's, his James Beard Award–winning restaurant on Bourbon Street.

The place was quiet at this time of day, before they opened later in the afternoon and welcomed customers until 3:00 a.m. Unlike the Windfall, the 24/7 casino he co-owned, which stayed hopping around the clock.

Overseeing operations, ensuring the sex trafficking ring ran without a hitch and the drugs flowed smoothly, and keeping a close eye on his business partner, Vincenzo Romero, demanded his attention the rest of his waking hours.

This was his one respite. From work. From his hostile partner, Enzo. From his clingy mistress.

In here, he could hear himself think.

He looked up from his computer as Colette, the hostess, strutted in carrying a tray with his lunch. A medium-rare rib eye and a side salad that he'd ordered in place of his regular fully loaded baked potato. He was trying to cut back calories lately. Slim down the waistline that'd only grown more robust with stress eating.

Colette had been there three years. Easy on the eyes

with a tight hourglass figure. She minded her business and earned extra by selling his drugs at the eleven universities in the area. A true hustler who never missed a day of work. He liked her.

She took the plate from the tray and set it down in front of him, along with ceramic salt and pepper shakers and utensils rolled up in a napkin.

He nodded his thanks.

"Can I get you anything else, Big Bill?" she asked in a tone that straddled the line between sweet and flirty.

He licked his lips as he undressed her in his mind. "A beer, sugar."

"Tommy is pouring it."

Even though Bill was cutting back and could forgo all the fixings, he wasn't giving up his Baltic porter. There were many things in this world he was capable of doing. Abstaining from sex and alcohol wasn't among them.

Colette flashed a small smile, tucked the tray under her arm and headed for the door. He loved watching her leave. Her body-hugging black dress fit her like a second skin, skimming all her curves, framing her nicely.

His gaze fell to his plate. Damn if that steak didn't smell delicious, but Bill had no appetite for it. The only thing he hungered for, the one thing that'd satisfy him, was Edgar Plinski's head on a silver platter.

Correction. Torturing that traitor for hours, *no, no, for days*, if they could keep him alive that long through the punishment Bill was going to mete out, *then* see his head on a platter.

Tommy Guillory, his right-hand man and his late sister Irene's eldest, walked in with the beer. His nephew's demeanor was low-key but could quickly shift to menacing, like flipping a switch. A good attribute for a gangster.

"Yo, yo, here you go." Tommy set the pint of dark, frothy porter beside the plate.

Bill shook his head. Today's youth had a flagrant disregard for old-school decorum. His nephew might be a classless millennial, but he loved the kid like a son. One day Tommy would run the organization.

"The game has begun," Tommy said, with the enthusiasm of a kickoff on Super Bowl Sunday, referring to the hunt for Edgar.

The news gave Bill a much-needed jolt of hope. "It's about time."

"D checked in." Frank Devlin was in charge of the secondary team. The fail-safe. "You were right, Uncle Bill. You won the bet." He reached into his pocket, pulled out a rolled-up wad of hundred-dollar bills and set it on the desk. "Those two Cajuns bit the dust."

The hit men brothers from the bayou were dead. They'd looked sharp enough, seemed capable and had an excellent reputation for specializing in Colombian necktie executions, but Bill had suspected that it'd take more than two backwater contract killers to get the job done.

Edgar was a slippery sucker, tougher to wrangle than an alligator and harder to hold on to than an eel in the dark.

But he wouldn't slip out of Devlin's snare.

Bill tugged on a self-assured smile. He was always right. Tommy was a fool to have doubted him in the first place and an even bigger fool to have taken the bet and staked his money on those bayou boys.

In his gut, Bill knew this would come down to the

A-Team. "Nothing wrong with outsourcing, but this is why it's important to have a contingency. Our local fellas will get the job done and collect the fee."

Ignoring the steak, he picked up the cash and tossed the roll in his desk drawer. Later tonight he'd give it to his little lady. He'd learned after two failed marriages to stick with a mistress who was young, had perky breasts, a firm backside and took more interest in shopping and staying pretty than in where his money came from.

That kind of curiosity could be used against him. The feds would jump on any weak link around him and crawl even further down his throat. They were already so deep in his gullet he was choking on their surveillance. Wiretaps on the phones. Spies in the casino. Bugs on the gaming floor and in the Windfall's offices. His every move watched by hawkeyed stalkers.

Besides his house, Avido's was the only other safe space where he could talk freely.

Tommy had the restaurant swept for surveillance devices *daily* before Bill set foot inside.

All Big Bill's men were absolute in their loyalty. Still, the only one he ever fully trusted was Tommy, since he was family.

"But it was good initiative on your part," Bill said, appreciating his nephew's gumption, "for thinking outside the box and contacting those Cajun *housepainters*." A euphemism for hit men who offed someone in their home. Quite acceptable to use around the little lady or in polite company without raising suspicion.

Tommy plopped down in a leather chair across from his desk, rested a booted ankle on the opposite knee and rubbed his bald head. Tall and thickset, the twenty-six-year-old kept his head clean-shaven to spare himself from getting the receding hairline that Bill had.

At fifty, Bill was too old and busy to fret over his lack of hair that emphasized the smooth cliff of his forehead and abundance of wrinkles.

"Do you think they'll bring him in alive or dead?" Tommy asked.

Bill wasn't a religious man and believed in no higher power than himself. Nonetheless, he was praying for alive.

His mouth watered to sink his teeth into Edgar. Literally. He wanted to rip off a body part Edgar would miss. Bill just hadn't decided which one first.

The depth of Edgar's betrayal was despicable. Unfathomable. What he had done was absolutely beyond the pale. Thinking of it, as Bill had endlessly done for the past two years, made his blood pressure skyrocket to the point his eye sockets ached.

It was a wonder he hadn't had a stroke.

Edgar had had a gambling problem and been in the hole up to his eyeballs. Two hundred and fifty thousand dollars. Edgar offered to work it off, using everything he knew about accounting, bookkeeping and tax laws. The proposal had possibilities, so Bill had taken him up on it. Recognized Edgar's true talent for balancing the books and hiding illegitimate activities under legitimate umbrellas without raising any red flags with the feds. Struck a gold mine. Introduced Edgar to some other outfits. Vouched for him as one of Bill's own. Claimed a sweet finder's fee. Had a really great thing going for everybody, especially for Edgar.

Then the weasel had got nervous about heat from the feds, jumped the gun and cut a deal.

But *the way* he'd left tore at Bill's heart every day… *Irene.*

The fallout was never-ending. If Edgar had evidence on two outfits, it was reasonable to assume that he had the goods on all of them.

Now every gangster Edgar had dimed out and every mafioso he'd done business with blamed Big Bill *big-time.* And each one of them wanted their pound of flesh.

Well, no way in hell was it going to come from him. *No sirree!*

Bill felt the vein in his temple bulge.

Money bought many things. Silence. Loyalty. But there was no amount in the world that'd buy a pardon for Edgar.

Or Bill. He'd tried and lost half of the Windfall. There was only one way out of this mess.

The vultures were circling, particularly Enzo, who wanted the entire casino, and Edgar Plinski would be on the menu.

He ground his back molars together so hard his ears rang. "Tell D and the boys, if they can bring him in alive, I'll throw in an extra mil."

"They're going to love the sound of that." Tommy clapped his hands, rubbing his palms together. "They expect to have him within the hour."

Restraining his excitement, Bill simply quirked a brow. "Pretty specific. Pretty damn confident, too."

"D wasn't pleased to hear about the bayou boys getting first dibs. Understandably so. But I think he was planning to let them do the hard part, then kill them and still collect the fee all along."

Nodding, Bill agreed. Sounded exactly like a stunt Devlin would pull. Tommy wasn't ever going to make it into Mensa, but he was sharp as a tack, had solid street sense.

"He took point on the traitor's house," Tommy continued, "to scope out the situation and had the others hang back. Well, those housepainters may have failed, but they set our home team up for success. According to D, the marshals assigned are some tactical special operators. Anyway, one of them is dead as a doornail."

"Really?" Bill picked up his glass and took a long pull on his beer. A small hum of appreciation slipped out at the creamy mouthfeel, decadent notes of coffee and chocolate, and the roasted malt finish. Delicious.

"That's not all." A wicked grin spread across Tommy's mouth, sort of diabolical, like that of a child tearing wings off flies. Without a doubt, Tommy had torn off wings and done far crueler things as a youngster. "You wanna hear the best part?"

Rather than respond, Bill shot him a scathing scowl. Rhetorical questions irritated him worse than sand in his sensitive parts. His patience was already threadbare, and this situation wasn't helping his volatile temper. He heaved a calming breath.

Tommy leaned forward, bringing closer a face only a mother could love—*God rest Irene's soul*. "The Cajuns caused such a ruckus that the marshals left their vehicle unattended long enough."

Okay, Bill would bite. "Long enough for what?"

"For D to do what he does best. Set the trap."

Bill's appetite flared up something fierce. He draped the napkin across his lap, grabbed the utensils and cut into his steak.

Good old Devlin. One of the Four Horsemen of the Apocalypse…and Bill's personal favorite.

War.

Chapter Four

What was so awful about a clean break when the alternative was to turn someone's life upside down?

Charlie wished Eugene hadn't felt compelled to talk to Sharon face-to-face and simply decided to leave. It would have been faster, easier and, yes, cleaner for everyone.

Sharon oversaw administration and personnel for the logistics services company her first husband started and ran until he died. The business managed the flow of goods and materials between points of origin and end-use destination, handling shipping, inventory and warehousing.

It also meant the company needed a lot of space at a reasonable price, which explained why it was located in the hills sandwiched between Tierra Santa and Mission Trails Regional Park.

In the middle of nowhere.

The good news was the traffic was sparse, making their travel time less than twenty minutes from the Palisades.

They passed the San Diego River and a few minutes later turned right off Mission Gorge Road into a parking lot. Torres brought the vehicle to a stop horizontally across a handicapped parking spot in front of the double doors that had the name Sullivan Logistics written on them.

"I've got this. Keep it running," Charlie said and hopped out.

She pulled open the front door and marched into the stark air-conditioned lobby up to the receptionist's desk. "Hello. I'm from the US Marshals Service. I need to speak with Mrs. Sharon Potter. It's extremely urgent."

After Charlie held up the badge that was prominently displayed from a chain around her neck, the twenty-something woman said, "FYI, she never changed her name from Sullivan to Potter."

One more anchor for Sharon.

Charlie's temperature rose. This trip was only going to eat up precious time.

In the end, Sharon wouldn't choose Eugene…Edgar Plinski over everything and everyone else in her life.

The receptionist picked up the phone and dialed. "Mrs. Sullivan, you're needed up front. A US marshal is here to speak with you. There's some kind of emergency." The young woman paused as she listened. "Okay." Then she hung up and looked at Charlie. "She's on her way."

Charlie nodded, stepping away from the desk, and put her hands behind her back. The at-ease position was an old Marine Corps habit that came naturally to her.

After serving eight years as a military police officer, living in the culture of extreme violence of the corps, doing merry-go-round deployments to Iraq and Afghanistan, she'd needed a change. Something different but still inside her wheelhouse. She considered working as a contractor or local law enforcement.

A chance encounter in a nightclub that'd turned into a two-night stand steered her in a new direction.

The guy was interesting, intelligent, noticed things most civilian guys missed, had a killer bod and carried a gun. He was a US marshal. In those earlier days, Charlie wasn't good with filler small talk after sex. Truth be told, she still wasn't. Fortunately, the marshal was. He didn't mind chatting about his job and had given her an inside perspective. She was hooked.

Once he discovered Charlie's hard-charging attitude and affinity for the grind of the Marines and military police, he'd suggested not only applying to the USMS, but also setting her sights on the Special Operations Group.

Now she had a job she loved.

Charlie glanced at the tactical black SUV, itching to leave. Rather than tap her foot impatiently, she paced around the wide lobby.

The sound of sensible pumps click-clacking across the tile floor snagged her attention.

An elegant, athletic-looking brunette in her early sixties, with bright eyes and gray at the temples, entered the lobby. She wore a silk blouse with a long, fancy scarf tied around her neck and slacks. "Excuse me, I'm Sharon Sullivan. Can I help you?"

"Mrs. Sullivan, I'm Deputy Marshal Killinger. I need you to come with me. Right now."

They'd already been attacked at the house. No way were they going to play sitting ducks twice in one day. Any talking would have to happen in the car and at the SSPC.

If Sharon later decided that erasing her past and forging a new life with Eugene wasn't what she wanted, the marshals would allow her to leave. But that discussion wasn't going to happen here at Sullivan Logistics out in the boonies.

"What is this about?" Sharon asked.

"Your husband. Eugene."

Her eyes grew wide and her hand flew to her chest. "Has something happened to him? Is he all right?"

"Mrs. Sullivan, is it okay if I call you Sharon?" The conversation in the car was going to be awkward. Calling her Mrs. Sullivan in front of Eugene would only compound things.

She nodded. "Yes."

"If you'll come with me, Sharon, I'll explain everything in the car." Charlie extended a hand toward the door, but the older woman stayed planted, as if rooted in shock.

"Please, tell me, what's going on?"

Charlie put a hand on her shoulder and gently coaxed her to start walking. "As soon as we're in the car."

The receptionist stood behind the desk. "Mrs. Sullivan, what should I tell everyone?"

"I'm not really sure," Sharon said. She stopped and looked from the receptionist to Charlie.

"Tell them there was an emergency. She'll check in with you later." Charlie held the door open. "This way, please."

Sharon walked across the threshold.

Charlie put a hand on her back, shepherded her the ten steps to the vehicle and ushered her into the third row.

"Honey, what's happening?" Sharon asked, confusion stamped on her face.

Eugene reached for her and helped her sit. "I'm so

sorry. I hate that you're being blindsided like this. I never thought this day would come."

Charlie climbed into the front seat, since Aiden's wound was bandaged. Torres whipped the car around into a U-turn and headed out of the lot.

"Blindside me with what?" Sharon asked. "Why are marshals here?"

"Sweetheart." Eugene kissed her hands. "I don't know what to say, where to begin."

"Sharon, your husband is in the federal witness protection program," Charlie said, cutting to the quick of it. If left up to Eugene, he might hem and haw all the way to the SSPC.

"What is she talking about, honey?" Sharon turned to Eugene. "How could you be in witness protection?"

"It's come to our attention that his life is in danger," Charlie continued.

"In danger? Oh, God. This is all so much. I don't understand. I thought witness protection made people disappear so they couldn't be found."

"That's correct, ma'am," Aiden said.

"Then how did someone find him?" Sharon asked.

"Yeah, I'd like to know that, too," Eugene demanded.

A fellow deputy in their field office had compromised the US Marshals Service. He'd accepted a bribe and handed over a classified Department of Justice laptop to the Los Chacales cartel. In turn, the cartel used the laptop to breach the Pacific Coast WITSEC list, along with the personal information of every marshal in California.

The ultimate betrayal of a colleague.

Justice was being served to the traitor, but the ripples

of his treason spread far and wide and deep. The cartel was now selling the sensitive information piecemeal.

Edgar Plinski wasn't the first with a bounty on his head and he wouldn't be the last. If the truth got out, panic and turmoil would infect every witness in the program like a disease.

Containing the news of the breach was crucial.

"The most important thing at the moment, Sharon, is the decision you're facing," Charlie said, doing her best to spin their attention in a different direction. "Very dangerous men know where your husband lives and about his current life. Which means they know about you, too. The only way we're authorized to protect you is if you choose to relocate with him, start over. New name. New history. No further contact with anyone that you know now."

Sharon gasped.

"We're taking you both to the Safe Site and Protection Center," Aiden said, "where you two will be able to talk and think in a safe environment. If you decide not to relocate with your husband, we'll take you to a relative's where you can stay, but you need to understand that unless you're in the program, we can't protect you."

Tension edged with fear radiated from the third row. The silence was agonizing because it was temporary. Charlie had never faced this particular scenario, where a witness had to be relocated a second time after marrying someone who had no clue he was in the program, but she guessed that any minute now there'd be weeping or screaming or both.

"What have you gotten me into?" Sharon's voice was brittle. Pained. "How could you put me in danger?"

"I was supposed to be safe and so were you." Her

husband ran his palms down her arms. "I'd never do anything to hurt you."

"Oh, Eugene." Sharon sobbed. "Is that even your real name?" she asked in a sorrowful whisper.

A crease formed between his eyes. He looked down, silent for several seconds. "It feels like my real name, but no, sweetheart."

"Who are you?"

"Edgar Plinski."

"Why are you in witness protection? Did you see a murder or some other crime?"

His shoulders slumped. "Something like that."

"You know how the program works," Aiden said, turning in his seat and facing the couple. "At the SSPC, the marshals are required to let her read your file. She has to know the truth so she can make an informed decision. That's how it works. Total honesty about who you really are and the things you did when a spouse is considering relocation. It's the only way to have a successful transition for all parties, whether you stay together or go down separate paths, where you never see each other again."

Brutal truth delivered in an environment where witnesses were on strict lockdown in forced proximity sounded like a recipe for murder, in Charlie's book. But managing the messy emotions of others wasn't her forte.

She barely dealt with her own. Better to tamp it all down, keep people at a distance.

Even Aiden. The one person in the world she was closest to.

"Eugene, were you some kind of criminal?" Sharon asked. "Or should I call you Edgar?"

"I prefer Eugene." He raised his head. His throat

bobbed on a nervous swallow. "I was an accountant. I didn't set out to be a criminal. I got roped into a bad situation. One thing led to another and I found myself getting deeper and deeper, until I felt like there was no way out. At least not alive."

A situation where he was complicit in tax fraud, sex trafficking, drug dealing, racketeering. The sordid laundry list was long, and Sharon would see every dirty detail at the SSPC.

"You lied to me. About everything," Sharon said. "Were any of the stories you told me about your past even true? Do you love me? Or were you using me to create your new identity?"

Eugene gaped at her and then snapped his mouth closed. He cleared his throat, a strangled noise that sounded as though he was choking on the answers.

Oh, hell. Not that Charlie had sympathy for criminals, but this predicament wasn't Eugene's fault. "He had to lie," Charlie said, throwing him a lifeline, hoping to defuse this inconvenient distraction. "It's part of the program. He wasn't allowed to tell you."

The tension started to deflate, and Charlie swallowed a sigh of relief, turning her focus on the road. No cars ahead in either direction. In the side mirror, the stretch of road behind them was clear to the bend, where she lost visibility farther back.

This full disclosure couple's session was making it difficult to concentrate on doing the primary job. Getting them to the SSPC was the priority. Not counseling them through this unmitigated disaster.

There were marshals with specialized training for that.

Sharon turned to her husband. "But I have no idea

who you really are, Edgar, who I married." Her voice was soft and forlorn.

"Yes, you do. You know me, sweetheart," Edgar pleaded. "We met in church because I became a born-again Christian. We fell in love because we share the same passions. Charity work and dancing and visiting vineyards and trying new wines. I love you. I love your kids. And the grandchildren."

Sharon burst into tears again. "Oh, the grandbabies. How can I leave them behind? And Cindy. She's due next month. I'm supposed to be there for them. They mean everything to me," she said, her voicing breaking. "My children are my life." She buried her face in her hands and sobbed.

A sudden stab of envy hit a sore spot in Charlie that she kept buried. There was an emptiness in her, a terrible aching void that'd never be filled. She'd never experienced what Sharon offered her family—the unconditional love of a mother.

Charlie's mom was a heroin addict, loved her next fix more than her children. Charlie and her sister, Britney, were shuffled in and out of foster care. Sometimes placed with different families. Sometimes in group homes.

Growing up that way had left her with a longing, a hunger and a pervasive fear of love.

As soon as Charlie was legal, she'd enlisted in the military branch that'd take her the soonest. She'd never gone back to Roanoke, Virginia. While Britney had never left. She became a stripper and married the first drunk loser to propose.

The only time Charlie heard from Brit was when

her ball and chain was fired from another job and they needed money.

"I'm so sorry." Edgar wrapped his arms around his wife. "If I'd thought it was possible for this to happen…" He dropped his head along with his voice.

No one in the DOJ thought it possible. Why would Edgar?

It was one thing when a person entered the program, preparing to testify. All newbies understood the risks and gambled that the government would protect them, since the alternative was far worse.

Edgar's story was a cruel anomaly. He'd crossed the threshold into a brand-new life, spent the past two years establishing roots and had finally stopped looking over his shoulder.

Believed he was safe only to find that he had to start all over again.

"I can't bear the thought of never seeing my family again," Sharon said, tears flowing down her cheeks. "My children. My grandchildren."

Family. Children. Grandchildren. Charlie's heart ached at the phantom pang inside her body. After suffering from endometriosis and failed rounds of medication therapy, she'd found herself unable to take the agony anymore. She'd been recommended a full hysterectomy by the doctor.

When Charlie woke up in the recovery room, she'd been surprised to find her mother had made the five-hour drive to the Naval Medical Center at Camp Lejeune in North Carolina. Charlie had been even more surprised at how glad she'd been to see her, clean and sober at her side.

Then her mother spoke, and the little miracle turned

into a nightmare. "The doctor says you're going to be fine. Surgery went well. I can't believe you let them take out your lady bits. You should've held out until you had children. Now you'll never be a real woman."

The bruising reality of those callous words had seared Charlie's heart like acid, scarred her soul in a way that she had never recovered from.

What Sharon had, four children, six grandkids, the love and warmth and security of a big, happy family, Charlie never would.

The unhealed wound she carried inside had grown bigger, deeper over the years as she tried to fill the emptiness with her career and ambition. With SOG. A unit that demanded the very best from her and the ability to drop everything and respond in six hours.

Old pain, still very sharp, sliced through Charlie. She gritted her teeth, cursing this assignment.

Being shot at and almost killed was part of the professional package, and she could handle it. But facing her personal demons was the worst torture. She'd choose waterboarding over this, no contest.

"You still haven't given me an explanation about how my new identity was blown," Edgar said, keeping an arm wrapped around Sharon. "I have a right to know."

"I'm afraid that's classified," Aiden said. "We're not authorized to share specifics."

"Then what guarantee do I have that it won't happen again?" Edgar asked.

Giving reassurances while holding their hand wasn't in their lane. At the SSPC, the other marshals would make it clear that he'd be relocated to a region in the program that was still *secure* and should never have to look over his shoulder again. More or less.

"You'll be briefed at the—"

Pop! Pop! Pop! Pop! The jarring sounds came from under the car. Tires exploding. A deep rumble. The slapping thud of rubber as the vehicle swerved. The shriek of metal grinding against asphalt.

Torres swung the car on the wide shoulder of the road near the river and brought the SUV to a stop.

Charlie's pulse skyrocketed as she gained her bearings. One *flat* tire might be an ill-timed accident. Two, possibly shot. But not all four decimated down to the rims.

Two black vans raced up to the shoulder. Ground to a screeching halt in front and behind them, bracketing the SUV, kicking dust in the air.

They were blocked in, sitting on rims, with nowhere to go besides the river.

Charlie pulled her 9 mm. Torres and Aiden did likewise. The Potters' panicked cries filled the cabin.

"Stay quiet!" Charlie said. The more noise they made, the more they were adding to the chaos and inadvertently helping their attackers.

The front doors of both vans opened. Four men wearing dark utility uniforms, bulletproof vests, balaclavas with skull faces, tinted goggles and tactical helmets jumped out. Each had a gun with a suppressor in their left hand. In their right hand was something else.

Something she never would've expected in a million years. Her brain cramped to make sense of it.

They surrounded the SUV, holding up paint sprayers. Cordless and high-powered. Ones you could easily pick up at any large home improvement store.

At the exact same time, all four men began spraying the bulletproof windows pitch-black, obscuring their vision. Blinding them. They couldn't even shoot out the windows.

Paint fumes flooded the car.

The Potters clung to each other. Edgar hyperventilated.

Sharon was hyperventilating. "God! We're going to die!"

The men had worked fast in a fluid, coordinated effort like they jacked marshals on the side of the road all the time as a hobby.

If it hadn't chilled her to the marrow of her bone, she would've been impressed.

The windows and both windshields were completely blacked out except for a four-by-eight-inch space on Edgar's windowpane. Where they taped something brick-shaped, covered in plastic wrap and attached to a timer.

"A bomb! Plastic explosives!" Edgar said, driving Sharon's screams to a fever pitch.

The countdown was at one minute.

They had to get out of the vehicle. There was no choice about that, but if they didn't go as a synchronized unit through the same exit point, firing simultaneously, they'd be hosed.

Everything transpired in only seconds. Gut-wrenching, terrifying seconds that made adrenaline course through her veins. In her mind, it all unfolded in slow motion.

Torres grabbed his door handle and pulled.

"Wait!" Charlie reached to stop him, but it was too late.

The driver's door opened. Torres hopped out and fired.

A flurry of gunshots from weapons with suppressors pinged. Torres caught a bullet in the throat and dropped.

Charlie trained her gun on the opening, not letting panic poison her. Air punched from her lungs. Her heart pounded in her throat. But she stayed sharp. Laser-focused. Ready for someone to shove the barrel inside, while keeping out of range and taking a potshot.

A loud champagne-cork sound echoed, and something was launched into the car, landing on the driver's seat. The door was kicked shut.

It was a familiar-looking canister. "Smoke grenade!"

Charlie dived into the back seat while Aiden leaped into action, climbing past Sharon and Edgar into the trunk.

"Sinaloa," he said, referring to a dicey mission in Mexico, where they had apprehended a fugitive. The circumstances had been much different, but a tactic they'd used would work for them now.

They were on the same wavelength. A single exit point for them both, but his idea was better. Smarter. She cracked a grin.

He was the best partner. The best outside-the-box thinker. The best friend.

The best everything.

"Stay put," Charlie said to the Potters, following Aiden into the rear of the vehicle.

"No!" Edgar grabbed hold of her leg as she maneuvered over the seat, and she had to knock his hands off.

The timer hit thirty seconds when the ballistic smoke grenade went off.

She held her breath, pressed up against Aiden in the sixteen cubic feet of space.

Red smoke suffused the tight quarters.

"Don't leave us!" Edgar coughed out the words.

Aiden hit the emergency latch, opening the trunk door. They rolled out, landing low on their feet. Smoke billowed around them, providing perfect camouflage to conceal their movements. Staying crouched low, Aiden broke to the left and Charlie went right.

As expected, each of the four gunmen was trained on one of the four doors, anticipating someone to leave from there. Not the trunk.

Charlie and Aiden had to press hard and fast to get the Potters safely out of the car and clear from the explosion within the next fifteen seconds.

Then the driver's-side rear door burst open.

Edgar jumped out and it all went to hell in a handbasket.

Chapter Five

Frank Devlin's plan was working without a hitch. Better than expected.

Eugene Potter, formerly known as Edgar Plinski, or *The Package*—as Devlin's team simply referred to him, removing the element of humanity—jumped out of the car, choking and gasping, right within arm's reach.

Thick red smoke blew from the trunk and rear door. No one had a clear, clean line of sight—most important, not the marshals.

Devlin didn't need one. He had The Package by the back of his shirt collar, holding him in front of himself like a shield with his Beretta 92FS against the base of the captive's skull.

But just because you didn't need something, it didn't mean you wouldn't be better off with it. Devlin and his team seized every advantage available, flipping down the thermal monocular strapped to their helmets, which allowed them to see through the smoke.

The wife stumbled out of the vehicle next, falling to the ground on her hands and knees. Tate, his buddy behind him, grabbed her and hauled her up onto her feet.

Devlin considered putting a bullet in The Package now and collecting two million dollars, split four ways, but why settle for two when you could have eleven? And at such a close range, it would make one hell of a mess all over him.

"We've got to move!" Edgar said, his arms flailing. "The bomb. Five seconds."

Devlin smiled behind his mask, so pleased with himself. "Three. Two. One."

Edgar covered his head with his hands, cowering, but there was no explosion.

Instead of using an expensive, volatile brick of C-4—that quite frankly wasn't so easy to come by—Devlin had covered basic silicone putty in colored plastic wrap. The timer sold the gambit. Made it imperative for the marshals to leave the vehicle. The smoke dialed up the pressure, fueled the chaos, stoked the panic.

"Package secure," Devlin said over the wireless communications devices his guys wore, keeping his gun pressed to The Package's head and his full attention on the blonde female marshal.

She was holding her position, using the rear of the vehicle as cover, gun raised. There was little else she could do, given the situation.

Layers of smoke rolling through the air obscured essential details, offering only glimpses. The Package was in his grasp. The wife was frosting on the cake.

Neither marshal would risk the shot.

The two others on his team came around the front of the SUV, their weapons aimed in the direction of the male marshal.

A silent, single tap on his shoulder told him his team had formed up and they were ready to move.

They backed away from the SUV toward the vans,

quickly but steadily, sure-footedly, out of the protection of the smoke.

A random passing police cruiser switched on flashing red and blue lights. Whipped around and stopped.

Without a word, Devlin's team changed their formation. They went from a horizontal line, trained only on the marshals, and shifted back-to-back, moving in a circle as one efficient unit. All the threats were covered before the patrol officer even left the car. It was second nature to them.

One of his guys popped more smoke toward the police car to cover their retreat.

"Freeze!" the cop said, crouched behind the door, his sidearm drawn.

The marshals hung back, using the cover of the SUV, but the smoke still put them at a huge disadvantage, clouding their field of view.

"Stop! Release the hostages," the officer said. "Lower your weapons and put your hands in the air!"

Devlin saw where this was going. Instinctively, he knew his guys did, as well. This wasn't their first rodeo.

"Stop!" the cop yelled again. "Or I'll shoot."

Unlike the marshals—highly trained, tactically skilled and wise enough to use a bulletproof vehicle for cover—the patrol officer was going to make a bad judgment call and would indeed shoot.

So one of his guys fired first.

A single bullet blew out the cruiser window and took the cop out of the game.

They reached the vans that they'd left running and peeled off into two groups. Devlin opened the sliding door and backed into the bed of the lead van with The

Package while Tate did the same at the other van with the wife.

Nothing like a solid day's work to energize Devlin. A mission like this always got the blood flowing.

The vans sped off, heading to the theme park. It was a twenty-minute drive or less from most parts of the city, making it a good spot to pinpoint in advance. From this part of town, it was less than fifteen minutes. They'd dump the vans and have their pick of vehicles to choose from, and it wouldn't be reported stolen for hours.

Devlin lowered to a knee beside Edgar. "You're going to die. Slowly. Painfully. There's nothing you can do about that."

"Please, no, no. Please."

He hated it when they begged. It never changed anything. Why not die with a little dignity?

"What you do have control over," Devlin said, "is whether or not you have to watch your wife get tortured first."

"Oh, God! She didn't do anything. She doesn't know anything."

"Like I said. Her fate is in your hands."

"What do you want?"

"Big Bill is under the impression you have incriminating evidence on him and his associates that you didn't turn over to the Department of Justice."

"Yes." The Package nodded emphatically. "Yes, on a flash drive. I protected Big Bill. I didn't rat him out. Please, don't hurt Sharon."

"Bill wants it." More like needed it. The noose was tightening around Bill's throat. It was the only thing that could save him from Enzo and the others. Maybe

Devlin would sell it for double to the competition. It was the golden ticket. "Where is the drive?"

"If I tell you where it is, do you promise not to hurt Sharon?"

"How about this? I promise that if you *don't* tell me, I guaran-damn-tee I *will* kill her. Where is it?"

"I don't have it." The Package lowered his head and wept like a baby. "The marshal, uh, the big guy with the bandage on his arm, took it. He's got it."

Devlin cursed and slammed his fist against the side of the van near The Package's head, making him cringe.

They had to turn around and go back. It was worth too much to leave the flash drive behind. They could pop more smoke, surround them and take them out.

"Hey, D," Tate said over comms. "We've got a serious problem."

Make that two problems. "What is it?"

"Those two marshals are following us in the cop car. Lights flashing."

Then the siren started blaring.

Fury pooled in Devlin's gut. It burned him to the bone that those two were in possession of the flash drive and would soon have every cop in the city chasing after them. With that kind of heat, they'd never make it out of San Diego.

They needed to find an alternate place to ditch the vans sooner than planned. In five minutes, SDPD would have a helicopter in the air and over their position.

First, he'd take care of those marshals. Teach them both a lesson they'd never forget.

"T, we no longer need the wife," Devlin said. "Injure her. Make it critical and toss her."

The Package's eyes flared wide in horror. "No! You can't. You promised you wouldn't kill her."

Devlin sighed. "I told him to wound her, didn't I? Not kill her."

Chapter Six

"Nice touch with the siren," Aiden said to Charlie.

He was kicking himself about losing two colleagues, plus Edgar and his wife, but it wasn't over. Not yet.

Charlie had been the first to make a beeline to the cruiser. When others might buckle and concede defeat, she bucked up and dug in for the fight.

She was relentless.

God, he loved her. Always had. Always would.

After they checked the patrol officer and saw he was dead, they took off in pursuit. Charlie had radioed in the incident to the police, giving the make and model of the vans, but there were no license plates. The cops' response would be faster and more widespread than the Marshals'—hot and heavy with one of their own gunned down. No mercy would be shown.

Aiden was closing the distance up to the rear van.

Only a few hundred yards separated them.

The sliding door slashed open. A face covered in a skull mask peered out, and then the man threw Sharon from the van.

Panic seized Aiden as her body slammed to the black-top, bounced violently several times and rolled to a stop on her back.

Those heartless bastards.

Aiden stomped on the brakes in front of the woman.

They both hustled out of the car and to her side. There were scrapes and bruises all over her, but her left thigh was covered in blood.

It didn't look like it had been caused by the fall out of the van.

Aiden peeled back the fabric where her pants had been torn. A fountain of blood spurted.

Jeez. The femoral artery had been sliced. This wasn't like the cut on his arm, something within their power to control. In three to five minutes she would bleed out. It could take that long or longer for an ambulance to reach them.

If they didn't get her medical help right away, she'd die here on this road.

That was what those men were counting on. Marshals giving up the chase to save a life.

"We've got to get her to a hospital or she's as good as dead," Aiden said.

He swore under his breath as they lifted Sharon up and carried her to the squad car.

"I think the closest hospital is off I-8," Charlie said. "Maybe ten minutes away."

That was the nearest hospital, but Aiden recalled seeing a smaller medical center on the map when they were going to get Sharon.

"There's one closer." Possibly five minutes. He hoped not any longer than that.

Gently, they got Sharon into the back of the vehicle.

Aiden took off south down Mission Gorge Road. Prayed his memory didn't fail him and he could navigate them there.

Charlie tore the sleeve from Sharon's blouse. Applied direct pressure on the artery.

"Tourniquet," Aiden said.

She nodded. "Okay. Yeah." Charlie took the scarf tied around Sharon's neck and wrapped it above the injury.

Good choice of material. For some reason on TV shows and in movies, people always used a belt. But a belt was too rigid, and you'd never get it tight enough to stop the arterial flow in the real world.

"I need a windlass."

A tourniquet without a windlass was a constricting band at best. Anything from a chopstick to a pocket-knife could be used. Aiden pulled a carabiner from his utility belt and handed it to her.

Charlie worked deftly. She held the tourniquet tight and kept up the pressure on the wound. "She's so pale. Hurry, Aiden."

He was going as fast as possible, taking bends in the road harder than he should.

"They didn't have to do this to her," Charlie said, her voice low.

No, they didn't, but it had worked. They'd known marshals would never abandon a wounded innocent. Aiden clenched his jaw and swallowed back the surge of white-hot anger.

They had to be close to the medical center. Sharon's life was literally draining away with each passing minute.

There. Set back off the main road about where he remembered from the map.

He saw a sign for the medical center that he'd overlooked before and took the turn. Followed the road and raced up to the emergency entrance, stopping in the ambulance parking area by a separate door.

Aiden flew out of the car and inside, grabbing the first attendants he spotted. "Help! There's a woman bleeding out. Cut to her femoral artery."

The orderlies got a stretcher and ran outside. Aiden helped them load her onto the gurney.

So much blood.

Charlie stayed at Sharon's side, going with them. Aiden killed the siren, lights and engine, and he sprinted to catch up to them.

By the time he did, after passing the treatment bay with curtains, Sharon was in a room for severe cases. A doctor and nurses swarmed around her, every medical person taking a specific action, each knowing exactly what job to do.

It reminded Aiden of the team that had attacked them. Precise. Prepared. Executed with ruthless efficiency.

"Excuse me," a nurse said to them. "We're going to need you to step out of the room." She ushered them into the hall and to the nurses' desk. "I need you to fill out some forms." The nurse reached behind the desk and proffered a clipboard.

Charlie looked down at the blood covering her hands and ballistic vest. The nurse directed her to the bathroom.

Aiden took the clipboard with a heavy heart.

"Also, her next of kin should be called," the nurse said.

"She's going to make it, isn't she?"

"We're doing everything we can for her."

Aiden called Sullivan Logistics and passed on the

tragic news to the receptionist, who assured him that she'd call her children immediately. Then he filled out what he could on the forms and returned them. "Her children are on the way. They'll have the rest of her information."

He paced in front of Sharon's room, watching the medical staff work on her.

Once the frenetic energy simmered down inside, the doctor stepped into the hall as Charlie came back from the bathroom.

"I'm Dr. Patel," the woman wearing green scrubs said.

"How is she?" Aiden asked.

"We've finally got her stabilized. The bleeding from the femoral artery is under control. She also suffered a severe head injury and has some broken ribs. I understand she was thrown from a moving vehicle at high speed?"

"Yes," Charlie said, her hands clenching to fists at her sides.

"She has swelling on her brain. The major head trauma has put her in a coma."

Aiden swallowed hard, his anger swelling.

"Is she going to recover?" Charlie asked, her expression tight.

"She's no longer in critical condition, but there's no way of telling how long the coma will last or if she'll wake up. We're going to send her for an MRI. Her family should get here as soon as possible. Excuse me." The doctor left.

One vicious act of cruelty and Sharon with her kind face, earnest eyes and fierce love for her family might never wake up. It was beyond unfair.

Two years ago, Aiden's mother had died after a painful battle with cancer. Where his father was the backbone of their large family, his mother had been the heart. With five kids, she always made each of them feel special and loved. Her last wish had been to die outside, under the sky. Not to be mourned, but to be honored, and for her children to live a full life.

Losing a parent wasn't easy, but to have them taken away by violence was unspeakable.

They'd failed to protect Sharon. This was their burden to bear, but that strike team had been a formidable force. Charlie tended to carry around guilt like sandbags. He didn't want that for her.

Aiden put a hand on her shoulder.

Charlie pulled away from his touch, pounding her fists against her thighs. "Bad things shouldn't happen to good people. I want to kill those men." She stalked off down the hall, storming through a set of double doors.

They'd get back out there, find Edgar and make those men pay for what they'd done. With any luck, the police already had them in custody.

Aiden went after Charlie, pushing through the doors. He walked down another hall, past vending machines and through another set of doors into the waiting room near the main entrance. The handful of people seated inside gave them a once-over, dismissing their weapons after noticing their badges.

Charlie stood still as stone, staring at the television mounted on the wall. He followed her gaze to the screen. Both of their pictures were featured on the breaking news.

"Two US marshals aided and abetted gunmen," the anchorwoman said, "in kidnapping a high-profile witness. In the process, they shot and killed a fellow marshal as well as a local police officer."

The bulletin was a punch to the throat.

Charlie muttered a curse. "This isn't good."

"That's the understatement of the century." Aiden grimaced at the television. "But I don't understand. We haven't done anything wrong."

"Not according to that." Charlie gestured to the screen.

"US Marshals Killinger and Yazzie," the anchorwoman said, "should be considered armed and dangerous."

What was happening?

Painful shock made Aiden's legs feel wooden. To have their names and faces splashed across the news was a gross violation of protocol.

The media could've only learned their identities from one person.

"We need to find out what's going on." Charlie gave a furtive glance around, prompting him to do likewise. "And why the police think we killed Torres and a cop."

"I'm sure our favorite person, Mr. Wonderful, would love to tell us." Will Draper.

Charlie groaned.

A little girl about ten years old was looking straight at them. Her gaze bounced to the television and then back to them. She turned to her mother, seated next to her with her face buried in a magazine, and tugged on her sleeve. The mother leaned closer, gaze glued to the article she was reading, and said something.

The little girl whispered in her ear as she pointed to the television.

"We can't hang around here unless we want to leave

handcuffed in the back of a squad car." Charlie nudged Aiden, guiding him through the double doors to the emergency room and around the corner out of sight.

Everything boiled down to two responses for Charlie—fight or flight. There was a time and a place for each, but if they weren't careful, they'd make a bad situation much worse.

This was a misunderstanding. It had to be the result of a breakdown in communication. "Before we make a rash decision that we might regret and run off half-cocked, we need to understand what we're dealing with first. Let me call Draper."

"Whatever he has to say, I'm sure it'll make my head want to explode." She drew in a deep breath. After a brief moment of hesitation, she nodded. "You're right. We need to know what's going on, but make it quick."

Aiden toggled his earpiece and dialed Draper's direct line. Unlike headquarters in Arlington, Virginia, and larger field offices, the San Diego office didn't have secretarial gatekeepers.

"US Marshal Draper," their boss said, answering his own phone.

"Sir, Aiden Yazzie here." He stared at Charlie as she tapped her Bluetooth comms device, conferencing in.

"Aiden?" There was a muffled sound and a quiet exchange as if the mouthpiece had been covered while Draper spoke to someone else in the room. "What were you and Killinger thinking?"

No mention of the witness or Torres. Not a good sign of how the conversation was going to go.

"Sir, we were about to call with an update when we heard there was an all-points bulletin out on us. What's going on?"

"I could ask you the same question. What happened out there? Did you two snap? Or are you doing it for the money?"

Charlie squeezed her eyes shut, frustration stretching tight across her face.

"We were doing our jobs. We had Albatross," Aiden said, using Edgar Plinski's code name, "and had just picked up the wife when we were ambushed on Mission Gorge Road. Torres was killed, along with a police officer that stopped to assist. Albatross was abducted and the wife was injured. She's in critical condition and the doctors aren't sure she'll pull through. But we had nothing to do with it, Draper."

"Nice touch on your part, trying to save the wife and calling in. It'd be enough to give me reasonable doubt about you two, if it weren't for the damning evidence against you."

Aiden's heart stuttered. "What evidence? We would never kill an innocent person, especially not a colleague or a police officer. You know us. You have to believe me."

"I believe money makes people do horrible things that they otherwise wouldn't. Before today, I would've thought you and your partner were the best marshals I had, but you wouldn't be the first ones in this office to sell their soul."

"Doesn't that say more about you than it does us?" Charlie snapped.

"Killinger." Draper sighed. "With a chip the size of an iceberg on your shoulder, perhaps I shouldn't be too surprised about you."

Charlie barely suppressed a snort.

Draper had some nerve, standing on his self-righteous

soapbox, spewing whatever garbage was going to help him sleep at night. There was absolutely no love lost for the man. Still, Aiden narrowed his eyes at Charlie. A silent warning not to get sidetracked.

"We're not traitors or murderers," Aiden said. "Why is there an APB out on us? Why do you think we killed Torres?"

"There was an eyewitness who saw it all and called 911."

Eyewitness?

Aiden sucked in a shallow breath, the taste somehow acrid, making his eyes burn.

Charlie slipped her hair behind her ear, her expression giving away nothing.

The bombshell unnerved her, too, although no one else would've been able to tell. Her Rock-of-Gibraltar demeanor appeared unflappable to the untrained eye, but Aiden knew better. Knew her well. The little hair tuck, a seemingly insignificant gesture, betrayed her emotions.

In that moment, she was feeling just as vulnerable as he was, even though she wanted the world to believe she kept her heart frozen in a block of ice. But when Charlie Killinger felt threatened, watch out. She became dangerous with a capital *D*. Went into take-no-prisoners attack mode, illustrating why a person should never corner a feral beast.

"That's impossible," Aiden said. His vision tunneled. "There were no witnesses."

"I guess you two weren't as careful about covering your tracks as you thought." The bitter accusation in Draper's tone was thick as ipecac syrup.

Aiden wanted to vomit. "Other than the police officer who stopped to help us, there was only a group of four guys who attacked us. There were no other cars on the road. No one else around." A strange numbness seeped through him.

Even if there had been someone, how could they have seen anything clearly through all the smoke from the grenades?

"Unfortunately for you two, that's not the case. Yazzie, you and Killinger disgust me. You should be ashamed of yourselves. As if this office didn't have a big enough mess to deal with, now you dump this in my lap. There's no way I can clean up this kind of nuclear fallout."

A tide of fury rose in Aiden, washing out his anxiety over being railroaded. Only someone as self-absorbed as Draper could turn this around and make it about himself.

"We called the police when we were tracking the men who abducted Albatross," Aiden said, "before they threw his wife out of a moving vehicle. Have the cops located the two black vans we reported?"

"There's no sign of those supposed vans. The chief of police is ticked that you had them spinning their wheels on a wild-goose chase when they should've been looking for you the entire time. Listen to me. Stay put at Mission Medical. Surrender your weapons to security. Cooperate with the police and go with them willingly. Don't endanger any more civilians."

The GPS trackers in their phones pinpointed their exact location. There was no doubt in Aiden's mind that as soon as Draper had been notified by the police, their boss had given them up without hesitation.

Not as if they'd been trying to hide. They'd taken the police cruiser of the dead cop to the medical center.

Charlie's gaze pinned him. Her cool, stony expression didn't waver, but he caught the flicker of fear in her piercing blue eyes as she took out her cell phone, removed the battery and smashed the screen against the wall.

A second later, she'd chucked it in the trash.

She was preparing to run.

There has to be another way out of this.

Charlie pointed to her watch, reminding him not to waste precious time if they wanted to avoid incarceration, and peeked around the corner. Whatever she saw, she must not have liked. Her index finger went up behind her back and she twirled it vigorously. The signal to wrap up, now, end the call.

"Draper, this doesn't add up." It didn't make any sense why anyone would falsely accuse them. "We're not guilty of this, and the real shame here is your utter lack of support."

There has to be another way out of this.

"I got an update right before you called. The eyewitness just arrived at the police station. He's seen pictures of you that I emailed after the chief of police notified me what was happening. The witness is swearing out an affidavit as we speak, identifying you and Killinger as cold-blooded murderers."

If there was another way out, Aiden couldn't think of it.

Chapter Seven

Two police officers entered the medical center through the main entrance and looked around the waiting room.

Charlie stepped back out of sight around the corner. "We have to get out of here."

Aiden hung up. "The dead cop was wearing a body camera on his torso. The footage should exonerate us. It'll show that we didn't kill him."

"We don't know what it'll show. There was a lot of smoke and he was hunched down behind his door. But they will have clear footage of me checking to see if he was dead. On the remote chance that it did clear us of his murder, it doesn't help us with Torres. Any time we spend in handcuffs, answering questions, is time lost to find Albatross before it's too late."

Aiden popped out the battery on his cell and tossed the phone in the trash bin. "We won't get far." He gestured to their vests and rifles.

They stood out like sore thumbs.

"Yes, we will." Determination fired through her veins. Surrender was not an option.

They'd been ambushed on an isolated strip of road where there hadn't been any CCTV. The two black vans had disappeared. There was an alleged eyewitness accusing Charlie and Aiden of collaboration and murder.

Only two people could clear their names. One was in a coma. The other was alive, but not for much longer.

They had to save Edgar. But first, they needed to get out of the medical center.

"Find the employee locker room and get us something to blend in," she said to Aiden, her pulse quickening. "Then meet me at the employee entrance."

No questions asked. No hesitation. He just nodded and took off.

That level of complete trust he had in her, and she in him, she'd never known with another soul, and she cherished it.

She went down a different hall back to the emergency room. When Sharon had been brought in, one of the nurses had run from the treatment room in the direction she was headed in now and returned with medication.

Another squad car with flashing lights pulled up to the ambulance entrance and parked behind the police vehicle they'd left. Officers rushed inside.

The emergency room buzzed with activity.

Staying close to the wall, she looked for the room she needed.

The officers were working their way in her direction, searching the emergency ward, pulling back curtains in the bay area. An infuriated nurse jumped in their path and read them the riot act about patient privacy.

The first room was no good—a janitorial closet. Neither was the second room. Nor the third.

One cop with a beard strode around the nurse and

moved in the direction of the treatment rooms, with his head on a swivel.

Her chest tightened. Any second, he'd spot her. As his head turned toward her, his hand on the hilt of his weapon, a large orderly stepped into his line of sight.

Charlie turned the next knob, opening the fourth door, and ducked inside. She breathed a sigh of relief. Finally, it was the one she wanted.

There were two refrigerators. Through the clear doors she saw vials of medication. Moving past the regulated drugs, she hurried to the shelving unit with medical supplies.

She quickly rifled through things and grabbed what she needed. Sterile gloves, gauze, saline solution, antibiotic ointment, topical anesthetic spray and a suture kit. Aiden's wound still needed stitches. They'd left all their supplies back in the·SUV.

Once they had a moment to catch their breath, she'd patch him up properly and make sure it didn't get infected.

She went to the door and pulled it open.

On the other side stood the bearded cop. He drew his sidearm.

Charlie shuffled back into the room, forcing him to follow her inside.

The officer stepped across the threshold, the gun leveled at her head, and let the door close.

A mistake. On his part.

"Hands in the air!" the cop said.

She dropped the supplies and did as instructed. Her small gesture of compliance emboldened him, made him think her arrest was in the bag.

"Turn around and put your hands on the back of your head," he said.

She didn't move. Didn't breathe. Didn't blink.

"Now!" His second mistake was getting close enough to touch her. He put his hand on her shoulder and tried to force her to turn around.

Charlie moved fast.

She snapped her hand up, catching the body of the pistol while shoving the muzzle sideways to keep her head out of the line of fire in case he pulled the trigger. Then she twisted the gun hard, not enough to break his wrist, just the right amount to sprain it badly.

The gun dropped to the floor.

The cop yelped, clutching his wrist.

Charlie kicked the gun, sent it sailing into a corner and threw her elbow into the side of the officer's head. A follow-up punch to the side of his neck and he fell into a boneless sprawl.

The neck was a vulnerable spot; you could crush a larynx or, as she'd done, deliver a sharp strike to the vagus nerve. At a minimum, it would cause disorientation. In the case of the cop, unconsciousness.

The emergency ward was crawling with police. For Charlie to get out, she needed to make herself less conspicuous.

Taking off her rifle, she grabbed two hospital gowns from the shelf. She threw one on like a coat, completely covering her back, and the second on the right way.

She took another, using it as a makeshift sack for her rifle and the supplies, and put on a white face mask.

Cracking the door, she peered into the hall. An officer was walking past the nurses' desk. She slipped out of the room and turned right, heading away from the cop.

Quickening her step, she shoved through a set of double doors and hustled down the corridor.

She glanced over her shoulder. The cop hadn't noticed her and was checking the rooms. Three more doors and he'd find his partner unconscious.

Charlie faced forward as she rounded a corner and slammed into a hard wall of muscle.

Aiden. Her throat loosened.

She hadn't heard any movement coming in her direction. His stealth never ceased to amaze her.

He was wearing scrubs over his clothes and carrying a gym bag that must've had his vest and rifle inside. "The cops have the employee entrance locked down," he said.

No. They had to get out of the medical center.

If they were arrested, no one would listen to them. Even Draper was ready to think the worst and he had known them for over a year, had witnessed firsthand their work ethic and integrity.

No one would believe anything they said, and Edgar would be tortured and killed.

Think. She had to think.

"There's another way, but we have to hurry," Aiden said, giving her a wild flash of hope.

He handed her a lab coat, scrub pants and a cap, then stuffed her makeshift sack into the gym bag.

They went down the hall as briskly and discreetly as they could, with her changing along the way. She ripped off the gowns, handed him her vest, which he stowed in the bag, and she put on the white coat.

As she finished shoving her legs into the pants and

put on the cap, a nurse came through a set of double doors. If the woman hadn't been looking down at her cell phone, she would've caught Charlie in an awkward position that would've been difficult to explain.

Charlie pushed the balled-up hospital gowns into the trash, and they passed the nurse, who was still preoccupied with her phone.

Aiden led her through a mini maze of hallways. They moved with confidence, acting like busy people who were supposed to be there.

They strode past a small elevator toward an unguarded door.

"That elevator goes directly to the maternity ward. This is a separate entrance for people with newborns, so the babies aren't exposed to germs. I overheard a nurse escorting a family through here." Aiden winked at her.

Warm pride filled Charlie's chest. He was brilliant. She wanted to hug him tight and kiss him. On the cheek only and not all over, she had to remind herself.

She was so attracted to him that it scared her. Attracted to the point where she worried that it distracted her on the job sometimes.

The moment they had first met, there'd been off-the-charts chemistry. Not a simple spark but a lightning bolt. And she knew he posed an indefinable threat. Whenever they'd got close to kissing or anything romantic, instinct cautioned her to keep away, the same sense of self-preservation that warned someone not to get too close to an open flame.

There was a line that she'd never cross. The problem was that the line with Aiden was drawn in sand, easily washed away by waves and redrawn. Sometimes it inched forward; sometimes it was pushed back. While knowing she couldn't have him made it worse.

The automatic door swooshed open. They stepped out together, breathed fresh air. The door sucked shut behind them.

"Now what?" Aiden asked.

"Leave that to me." Charlie gestured for him to follow her. "I'm going to hot-wire a car."

"What?" The surprise in his voice matched his expression. "Why am I just now learning that you even know *how* to hot-wire a car?"

She shrugged. "I guess it's the first time I've needed to do it." As an adult. "We'll need to find an older model." Those were easier. "Ten years at least, but the older the better."

"If we wander around, checking vehicles, we'll look like car thieves."

"We are car thieves." She'd never thought the day would come when she'd say such a thing, and definitely not to Aiden Yazzie, the most upstanding, principled man she knew.

There was a parking lot to the left, across a wide expanse of blank blacktop, in full view of several police officers. They rounded the corner to the left.

Ahead of them was the smaller parking lot for employees. A guy got out of a luxury sedan and hit the key fob, locking it. The lights flashed and he tossed the keys in the right pocket of his suit jacket. Looking frazzled, the man jogged toward an entrance, where one police officer was busy on his radio.

"Better idea," she said. "Head to that sedan. I'll meet you."

They separated. Aiden quickly disappeared among the other cars in the lot.

Charlie picked up her pace, putting herself in the man's path. As he was about to pass her, she bumped into him, slipping her hand into his pocket and grabbing the keys tight in her palm, without letting them make a sound.

"I'm so sorry," she said.

"No, excuse me." He gave her a hurried look-over, but kept going, none the wiser.

By the time Charlie had reached the car, the man had already cleared the cop and was in the medical center. She hit the key fob button. The car lit up inside, turn signals flashed once and the door locks clunked open. They climbed inside, and he threw the bag in the back.

She pushed down on the brake, pressed the start button, got the engine going and pulled out of the lot.

Charlie went west on the side street, at a speedy but not suicidal pace, as if they were late for an appointment, past a market and veterinarian and eateries. At Mission Gorge Road, she made a left, going south.

A *thwopp, thwopp, thwopp* sound had them both peering low through the windshield and up at the sky. A police helicopter was inbound, heading to the hospital.

Farther down the road, on the opposite side, a string of police cars raced north. Lights flashing. Sirens blaring.

At least ten squad cars flew past them.

The police would have the entire medical center locked down and under aerial surveillance within minutes.

They'd made it out in the nick of time.

"We need cash," Charlie said. They wouldn't be able

to use credit cards since those left a digital trail anyone could follow. "Then we need to get a car that won't be reported stolen."

She drove to Seaport Village. A fourteen-acre waterfront complex of shopping, dining and entertainment. The meandering walkways and beautiful plazas attracted tons of tourists and locals. It also had one of the few banks in the city with ATMs inside that allowed up to a three-thousand-dollar cash withdrawal.

The police would eventually monitor the activity of their credit and debit cards, but for right now, the cops thought they were pinned down somewhere inside the hospital. On the off chance that they were already plugged into their financial transactions, it would be easy to hide in the crowd and disappear. It wasn't as if they were going to hang around the area waiting for the police to arrive.

She parked the sedan as close to the bank as she could while staying away from CCTV cameras. It was impossible to avoid all the cameras between the parking lot and the bank, but every little bit of prevention helped.

In case the car was reported stolen sooner rather than later, they decided to ditch it. Aiden grabbed the bag from the back. They hustled to the bank and both made withdrawals, not knowing how much money they might need.

Better to have too much than not enough. This was their one chance to get cash.

On the way out, she spotted the Green Line trolley pulling to a stop.

"It'll take us where we need to go." She pointed to it.

Aiden nodded and they ran, hopping on board just before it pulled off.

"Whose car are we taking that won't be reported stolen?" Aiden asked, whispering in her ear.

"Someone who won't miss it."

Nick McKenna. Fellow marshal and former lover, currently out of town visiting his girlfriend, Lori Carpenter, who happened to be in WITSEC. They'd fallen in love on a yearlong assignment where he'd protected her.

A solid, stand-up guy, Nick could be relied on in a pinch. At least Charlie hoped so, considering their baggage.

Before she joined the SOG and was assigned to San Diego, she'd been at the Omaha field office. Her work relationships there had got so ugly they'd become toxic. When a woman slept with multiple colleagues—it was a small town and choosing lovers from the work pool was pragmatic—she developed a reputation that a man never would've had to contend with.

San Diego was a fresh start. She'd been careful. Then one night after dinner and drinks, she'd wanted Aiden so badly she ached. But what she shared with him was the most important relationship in her life, and she wasn't going to spoil it acting on an impulse that they'd regret.

So she'd taken the convenient bait of Nick's overtures and gone home with him.

A stronger woman, a better woman, a sober woman would've picked a random stranger. Someone anonymous. Someone disposable.

It had been fun, casual, easy, until she realized it had been a lie. Nick wasn't capable of emotionless sex. To him, none of it had been casual. Or easy.

"We're going to take Nick's truck," Charlie said.

A muscle jumped in Aiden's jaw. If she'd blinked, she would've missed it.

"What is it?" she asked as he straightened away from her. "What's wrong?"

Chapter Eight

Aiden reined in the sudden storm of emotions rolling through him, locked them up tight and washed his expression clean.

The day Charlie had been assigned as his partner and they'd shaken hands, the rush of endorphins was immediate, the attraction visceral. He'd been in a relationship at the time, but the more he got to know Charlie, slowly over time, the less he could silence the little voice whispering that she was *the one*.

So he'd broken it off with the other woman. Believing it was only a matter of time for him and Charlie until their point of happy confluence and they'd be together.

"What is it?" Charlie asked. "What's wrong?"

Every single detail from that night in the restaurant was burned into his memory. The flush on her cheeks from the alcohol. Candlelight on the table sparkling in her animated eyes. He'd put his palm on her thigh and she'd leaned into his touch, pressed her cheek to his. The way she'd smelled of wild summer flowers, the warm heat of her breath on his face. He'd caressed her jaw, her skin was delicate, soft, and every atom of his being screamed *kiss her*.

Then she'd straightened away from him, as if waking

from a dream before he could, and gone to the restroom. He'd wrestled with his feelings and what to say, not wanting to still be stuck as just a *friend* in the morning.

Aiden wasn't interested in a brief fling with Charlie. He wanted forever.

But she'd never made it back to the table. Nick had found her at the bar, or she'd found him.

Either way, Aiden wouldn't think of the devastation.

He recalled happy things instead—riding a horse with the wind in his hair, making it through SOG training, the sound of his nieces and nephews laughing as they played—and pulled on a soft grin.

"Nothing's wrong," he said, doing his darnedest to sound laissez-faire. "It's smart." And it was. "Nick won't miss his car while he's curled up in bed for a week with Lori." Aiden watched, waited to see if an ember of jealousy sparked in her.

Charlie didn't bat a lash. "My thoughts exactly."

He wasn't sure which hurt more. The fact she'd slept with someone in the office, his friend Mr. Dark-and-Stormy with that carved-in-stone jaw, or that it had meant so little to her.

Nick was everything Aiden wasn't. A super serious loner, choosing a scowl over a smile. Hotheaded and impulsive to a fault. In many ways, Nick was like Charlie.

Aiden thought the fling would've lasted two nights, two weeks at most.

It'd gone on for two months.

Two months of dinner and drinks and public displays of foreplay. Two months of watching Nick's infatuation grow while Charlie maintained her "touch, but don't feel" approach, guarding her heart like the gold reserve at Fort Knox, and Aiden played man-trapped-in-the-freaking-middle.

Sixty-five days of torture.

Charlie had been blind to the pain it caused Aiden. She still was. In her defense, he worked very hard to blind her.

She wasn't property that he owned. They were friends, close as family. She had a right to sleep with whomever she chose without a guilt trip, without pettiness, without judgment on his part.

Aiden only wished she had chosen him.

They got off the trolley in the Gaslamp Quarter, two blocks from Nick's apartment building. The urban center was the heartbeat of the city.

Aiden preferred his tranquil condo overlooking the water. There he had peace of mind and the quiet to reflect.

Whereas Nick enjoyed the hubbub with energy always circulating, always something to do to keep him from thinking about life. Perhaps that was why things had lasted so long between Nick and Charlie. They'd been objects in constant motion bouncing between work, activities down at the Seaport, entertainment here in the Gaslamp Quarter, which turned into a playground for adults after dark, and then off to the bedroom.

Pushing it from his mind, Aiden followed Charlie into the residential parking garage. They walked to Nick's designated spot and found his Dodge Ram.

"Can you break in without smashing a window?" Aiden asked her.

"No need." She dropped to the ground by the front wheel on the driver's side and felt around for something. "Bingo."

Charlie stood, holding a magnetic key box. Inside was an extra fob.

Aiden had no idea it was there. Nick was like a Boy Scout, always prepared, but it was salt in the wound realizing that his buddy and his best friend—the woman he loved—knew things about each other outside the bedroom that Aiden didn't.

The stab of longing and jealousy in him was sharp.

No way was he delving toward things inside the bedroom.

Aiden tossed the bag in the back. They stripped off the scrubs and he got behind the wheel, firing up the fully gassed truck.

They took I-8 East. The first step was to get out the city, then the state.

"We need to find Albatross," Charlie said. "Finish what we started."

It was their duty to save him, if they could, but it went deeper now. "As well as clear our names. Everyone believes we're guilty because of this alleged eyewitness. I can't wrap my head around it."

"Pretty convenient, isn't it?"

"Too convenient. Too tidy." The whole thing reeked.

"Do you still have the hit man's burner phone?" Charlie asked.

"Sure do."

"Can I have it?"

Aiden dug in the pocket of his jeans and handed it to her. "What are you thinking?"

"We need to know who is accusing us, but we'll need a little assistance to find out."

"Draper won't lift a finger to help us, and no one else in the office is going to be inclined to stick their neck out. Not with this kind of heat. If Draper found out, he'd tank their career."

"There's one person who might help us." Charlie shifted in her seat, turning to him. "Nick."

Aiden was quiet for a long moment. Shame swept through him as he remembered the resentment that he'd held against Nick during those two agonizing months.

"On vacation, he can help from a distance," Charlie added. "He hates Draper just as much as we do, probably more, and is already planning to transfer to another office. I think he's our best chance to get some answers."

The reasoning was solid. Unable to find fault with it, Aiden nodded. "Call him."

"Maybe the request would be better received if it came from you."

Nick had moved on; he was no longer hurt by the way Charlie had treated him, and he was in love with Lori. Even better, the one thing his buddy couldn't resist was a woman in trouble.

"You call him," Aiden said. "Nick has a serious savior complex." Maybe Nick thought he could save Charlie from a loveless, lonely life. But Nick didn't understand that she didn't need to be rescued. Charlie had to be the hero in her own story. Fear was her dragon to slay. Love was her choice to make. No one could do it for her. "It's a big ask, but he won't say no to you. Trust me."

"What's his number?"

"You don't have it memorized?" Aiden asked, keeping his tone light, teasing.

A hint of a smile played over her lips, her eyes deadly serious. "The only number I have memorized is yours."

That was music to his ears. Aiden rattled off Nick's number.

"I hope he answers, since it'll be an unknown number," Charlie said.

He hoped Nick wasn't too busy making love to Lori with his phone shut off. Nick had only landed in Phoenix today. It'd been weeks since he'd seen Lori, and he must've missed her something awful.

Aiden was happy his friend had finally found happiness.

Charlie dialed and waited with the phone to her ear. Nick must've answered, because she put the call on speaker. "It's me, Charlie. Aiden and I are in a world of trouble. We need your help."

"What do you need?" Nick asked, without a beat of hesitation.

The man was a good friend and a great marshal.

Charlie explained the details of the situation. "According to Draper, the eyewitness is making a formal statement. We need to know who it is. Figure out a motive. Maybe discredit the person."

"I know Albatross," Nick said. "I was the one who got him settled in San Diego and helped him with his transition. I might reach out to someone in our office for information, claiming I saw it on the news. I also have a reliable contact in the SDPD."

"Since you knew the guy and you're familiar with his history, do you remember anyone who might've had a grievance against him?" Charlie asked. "Or anything odd about his case that stood out?"

"As a matter of fact, yeah. The US attorney's office was livid at first. They were expecting information on one mobster they'd been going after. Some guy in New

Orleans—uh, I can't recall the name. Anyway, Albatross had been working closely with him, was even engaged to his sister, I think, but in the end, Albatross gave them nothing on the target. Instead, he turned over evidence on two other big fish. Two convictions versus one, so the US attorney's office accepted it and made the deal."

"That's helpful, Nick," Aiden said. "More than you know. Thanks for helping us. We really appreciate it, brother."

"No problem. You'd do the same for me. When I get something, should I call this number?" Nick asked.

"Yeah, this number." Charlie lowered her head and her voice went soft. "Thanks, Nick. And hey…the way things ended between us, I, uh, I—"

"There's no need to apologize. It doesn't matter anymore," Nick said. "It was a long time ago, and I found what I was looking for with Lori. We're getting married."

A strange tension blasted off Charlie as she sat back in the seat.

Things had broken off badly between Nick and her.

Nick had ended the fling once he realized he'd never be anything more than entertainment for her, a diversion, a toy, and Charlie had lost it because Nick had beaten her to the punch. But no matter how ugly the breakup, Nick had defended her against others in the office who had snide, unkind things to say about her, and he had even broken one marshal's jaw.

Hotheaded and impulsive, but Aiden respected the heck out of Nick for it.

"Okay. Thanks. We appreciate the help." Charlie disconnected.

That wall of hers went up, like an iron curtain drawn between them, and Aiden felt lost. She hadn't cared about Nick, not romantically, but something troubled her.

"Does it bother you that he's getting married?" Aiden asked. "You're not jealous, are you?"

"Of course not." The stark sincerity in her voice relieved him. "It's just that… Nothing." She shook her head. "It's stupid."

"Nothing you have to say is stupid. What is it?" He glanced over at her.

There was a glimmer of pain in her eyes—just a flash like lightning in the darkness—and then it was gone. "The only reason I let it last so long with Nick was that I thought he was like me. That hooking up was enough. That he believed happily-ever-after was a crock," she said, a cutting edge to her voice. The normal confidence she carried faltered. "He pushed for me to spend the night, leave stuff in a drawer. And I thought it was about him needing to control a woman who refused to be controlled. Turns out that he really does want the lifelong commitment, house with white picket fence, two-point-five kids."

Sounded pretty good. Aiden wanted to get married, settle down, have kids, build a home like his parents had. Only problem was he couldn't envision it with anyone other than Charlie.

"What's wrong with wanting that?" Aiden reached for her hand and took it in his.

She flinched and he closed his fingers more firmly around hers, expecting her initial reaction.

"For every nine out of ten people who want it, are drawn to it, one isn't. Or can't have it. For every nine out of ten who run toward the dream, one is stuck with reality. I guess I'm that one." She pulled her hand away from his, shifting in her seat, and cleared her throat. "Do you think the men who attacked us are going to take Edgar to New Orleans?"

Aiden's head spun as he tried to keep up with Charlie's dodge-and-evade maneuvers.

There were times such as now, when she'd give an inch and he wanted to press for a mile through that thicket of thorn bushes surrounding her, needing to delve deeper so badly regardless of the injuries he suffered. But he'd get better results beating his head against a wall than taking a battering ram to her heart.

In the wake of his silence, she said, "504. That's the area code of the number that texted the hit men. New Orleans, right?"

Her emotions were compartmentalized and controlled to the point of strangling. She radiated a distance that was part of her core. She wore that cold bravado like armor.

One of the things Nick had grumbled to Aiden about Charlie was the lack of closeness. Nothing physical that wasn't foreplay, culminating in cool, no-nonsense sex. No hugs. No kisses beyond flirting. No postcoital cuddling. No sharing of anything of substance.

Nick's complaints had left Aiden mystified.

In those quiet moments between Aiden and Charlie, when an intimacy was tangible and a physical kind seemed possible, she shared bits of her childhood, glimpses of her soul. There was no doubt in Aiden's mind that hidden behind her cold reserve, she had an inner fire that raged, burned so hot that it would scald.

Sadness leaked through him at the absence of tenderness and affection in her life. He ached to give her the emotional warmth and security she deserved, to feed her heart and soul.

He gripped the steering wheel harder with both hands and took a deep breath. "Yeah, that's the area code for New Orleans. The hit on Albatross feels personal, with the offer of extra money to bring him in alive so he could be tortured. With the involvement of the mobster's sister and the fact that Edgar had worked closely with that guy, I'd say it's our best lead." The only thing they had to go on.

"It would be impossible for them to fly there with a hostage. They'll have to drive. How long do you think it'd take them to get there?"

Aiden had mapped out the drive from San Diego to Camp Beauregard in Pineville, Louisiana. Twenty-four-hour trip that he could make in two days, if he took the job. Tack on an extra four hours to get to New Orleans.

"I'd estimate twenty-eight hours," he said. "They'd drive straight through in shifts, only stopping when absolutely necessary for gas, food. Maybe twenty-nine hours if we're lucky."

"We need to beat them there, be ready once they arrive and find Albatross before they kill him. But with the head start they have on us, the only way to do that is to fly."

"Have you forgotten we're wanted? They'll be on the lookout for us at airports."

"I agree that trying to fly from any airport in California would be suicide." Charlie stretched, rolling her shoulders, and Aiden could hear the wheels spinning in her head. "Didn't you mention that on the reservation there are independent Navajo-controlled airports?"

"Yeah, so?" he asked, not liking where this was headed.

"So, your father is an important man."

Aiden's dad was the chief of a tribal council. He was essentially a governor with executive power, and the council had legislative power.

The position was one of great respect and influence.

"If you called him," Charlie said, "and explained the situation, don't you think he'd get someone to do him a favor? Get us on a flight to New Orleans. With our weapons. No IDs needed. No questions asked. He would gladly help."

Without a doubt, his father would help any of his children in need, but Aiden would never ask such a thing of him. Charlie should've known better than to suggest it, but her upbringing was so different. Aiden's family was large and tight-knit. Honor and respect and principles were as important as love.

Charlie didn't speak to her mother anymore for some reason and only exchanged a few hollow pleasantries with her sister around the holidays. She'd never been taught the value of family, the sanctity of such a bond. All she knew was the anger, the fear and loneliness from not having it. He understood that was the reason she held herself at such a distance, but he was no longer sure she'd ever let him in on the other side of her wall.

"No," Aiden said, shaking his head to emphasize his point.

"Why not? It'd be easy."

"The easy way isn't always the right one. I won't ask my father. You don't use family like that. Not if you care about them. This is our problem. I won't drag him into this."

"Your family is off-limits, but it's fine for us to get Nick involved? He might only be getting us information, but we're also making him complicit. He's aiding and abetting us. I guess that double standard sits fine with you."

The hypocrisy of it twisted through Aiden's chest. Charlie's point was valid.

Growing up, he'd worshipped his father. He'd been taught to protect his family at all costs.

Nick understood the stakes, the risks, and knew that if the shoe was on the other foot, he could rely on them to stick their necks out the same way for him. Nick could've said *no*, whereas Aiden's father wouldn't have a choice. His dad would be compelled to help.

There was a fundamental difference that he couldn't put into words.

Folding her arms, Charlie looked out the window and dropped the issue.

A heavy silence filled the confines of the cab, almost consuming them in its enormity.

Aiden flipped on the radio and tuned in low background noise. He upped the speed a bit, keeping it under the limit. They didn't come this far to get stopped for a traffic ticket.

For a hundred miles they drove east toward the mountains and the Arizona border without talking. There'd never been the need to force chitchat between them. It always flowed. The quiet moments were natural, not awkward and uncomfortable as it was now.

Her stomach growled, but she said nothing.

He saw a billboard for a shopping mall and restaurants. They both had bloodstains on their jeans. Most people might overlook it, but a keen eye would find it suspicious. If they figured out a way to fly, they couldn't go through an airport looking like this.

Taking the off-ramp, he pulled into Yuma, five miles across the Arizona state line. First, he stopped for gas, making sure to keep his face turned away from the cameras.

Then he found the mall, which wasn't hard. It was a sprawling, palm-tree-studded outdoor complex with plenty of stores to choose from, dining options and a theater.

He parked at a department store. "We should get fresh clothes," he said.

"Good idea."

Inside, Charlie headed to the women's section and he went to the men's.

Under normal circumstances he'd gravitate toward the sales, but efficiency was his focus. They needed to get in and out. He browsed quickly and found a replacement pair of jeans. Dark wash. Perfect size in a brand he was familiar with. Fifty bucks. His shirt was in good condition, but after smelling under his arms, he searched for something new. He grabbed a moisture-wicking crew T-shirt that had the stretch and fit he preferred, navy instead of black, and a long-sleeve button-up shirt to wear open and hide the bandage on his arm.

He changed in the cubicle, trashed his old stuff and took the tags to the checkout. Near the register, he saw a ball cap and grabbed it, too. His total was a hundred and twenty dollars.

It took them ten minutes to meet back up. Charlie wore slim-fitting jeans that looked great on her and a V-neck T-shirt in light gray that hugged her curves and flat stomach. She'd also added a cotton warm-up jacket.

"Hungry?" he asked.

"Starving."

In-N-Out Burger was a close walk and the food would take no time. They ate inside, their backs to a wall, away from cameras and other people.

Charlie took a bite and moaned. "This is the best burger ever."

Digging in, he had to agree. After the day they'd had and three hours hauling butt to get out of California, they were both famished, and almost anything would've tasted good, but the thick patty and cheese and grease hit the spot.

"You never did tell me where you learned how to hot-wire a car and pick pockets," he said.

"In a group home. The place was like a jail, with white concrete walls and bedrooms that resembled cells. They even had rules against hugging because it violated the no-physical-contact policy. Some of the girls in there were on the road to becoming criminals. I picked up those skills from troubled kids, to pass the time, for fun. Other things I had to learn to survive. Like how to fight. To make sure that if I let the other girl get back up, I taught her a lesson first so she'd never touch me again. It wasn't an easy place to grow up. But in there I figured out how to turn my anxiety into anger, channel it into something useful."

He knew about her mom's drug problem and Charlie's time in foster care, but he'd thought it had been a brief stint. "How long were you in the system?"

"My sister and I bounced in and out from elementary to high school."

Her most impressionable years had been spent in an institutionalized environment with child welfare monitors instead of loving parents. His heart sank. It pained him to imagine it.

"Why didn't you ever tell me all of this?" He opened his water bottle and took a long draw.

She shrugged. "I guess I don't like thinking about it. All of your childhood stories are wonderful."

"That's not true." He'd shared his tough lessons and disappointments. The racism and stereotypes he had to endure outside of Navajo Nation. His world wasn't sunshine and rainbows every second of the day.

"Okay, you're right. That's not fair. But I don't really have any happy stories. With the stuff I learned in the group home, being in that environment, I could've just as easily ended up like my sister instead of..." Charlie lowered her burger, her gaze darting around. "I have an idea. I know how to get us on the plane. I'll be right back."

She wiped her mouth with a napkin and went up to a male employee mopping the floor.

A young guy in his early twenties. Laughter flowed back and forth. Then he wrote something down on a piece of paper and handed it to her.

Charlie waved bye to the kid and came back to the table. "Let's go."

They grabbed their burgers and drinks and got into the truck.

"We need to go here." She handed him the slip of paper.

"The Oasis. What is this?"

"The solution to our problem." A bright smile spread across her face, lighting up his heart. "Drive."

Chapter Nine

The atmosphere of the Windfall Casino on Fridays was an appealing balance of electric and calm. One of Big Bill's favorite things to do was stroll around undisturbed by anyone for a few minutes and take it in as a tourist might, but he could never shut off his managerial brain.

Dressed to the nines as usual, he wore a quiet dark suit, a perfectly laundered shirt, an elegant silk tie and gleaming black oxfords. First impressions mattered. He could intimidate a person, get inside their head and establish the pecking order simply with his attire, without uttering a word.

Bill walked through the main downstairs gambling room. It was filling up. By nine tonight, it would be packed.

He cast his gaze across the slots. Two-thirds of them were taken, a mix of men and women, most over forty, a relatively shabby bunch that'd stay planted well into the wee hours. The blackjack and craps tables and roulette wheel were in good use.

Bill had got his start in Las Vegas and risen through the ranks from croupier to pit boss to manager. Hustling was in his blood. He'd seized every opportunity to advance, even if it meant getting his hands dirty. *Bloody* would be more accurate. Notorious mobsters were responsible for making Vegas what it was today. Bugsy, Lansky, Luciano...

Those old-school greats had shaped Sin City. They'd given Bill the vision to one day go back home to New Orleans and open a casino of his own. Plunder an untapped market. Build a legacy for his family. With no children of his own, this would one day go to Tommy. He was as good a son as any who might have been his.

There were other casinos in the state on floating boats and at the horse-racing track with slots, but the Windfall—Big Bill's masterpiece—was the only land-based private casino with table games in the state. Louisiana law provided for fifteen riverboat licenses but only one land-based. Plenty of others had applied, but Bill had shed a lot of blood and greased a lot of palms to make sure the Windfall won.

Now he had to fend off greedy interlopers like Vincenzo Romero, who coveted what Bill had built. They thought they could take it by putting a knee to his throat and applying pressure.

All because of Edgar.

Bitterness filled Bill's mouth. He had turned a down-on-his-luck accountant into the Money Magician, like turning polluted water into wine. Bill had even set him up with his younger sister, Irene, thinking they'd make a nice match.

And what did that dirty dog do?

Stabbed Bill in the back...and killed Irene on the way out the door.

Pain squeezed his heart, rage setting his blood on fire. For a moment, he shut his eyes in quiet misery. Bill had never imagined that Edgar was capable of murder, but he'd never underestimate him again.

Suffering was in store for that two-faced, double-dealing liar.

A comeuppance was due, and Bill was going to make sure Edgar got it. Slowly. Painfully. He'd make a list of Edgar's body parts to hurt and check it twice once that man was kneeling in front of him, begging for forgiveness.

Enzo strutted past the roulette wheel, wearing a two-thousand-dollar suit, shaking hands and kissing cheeks as if the 51 percent stake in the Windfall that Bill still owned was already his.

They were roughly the same age, had started making their mark about the same time, and both had ambition in spades. Enzo dyed his gray hairs and kept a trimmer physique, but the crucial difference was his deep familial connections in the syndicate supporting him.

A type of protection Bill lacked.

Bill had created this on his own, from nothing. Losing it because of Edgar, a man he'd protected, vouched for, had almost considered family…a man who'd killed Irene, was unconscionable.

Such a betrayal couldn't go unpunished.

Seething, Bill headed for the poker room.

Twenty tables open 24/7, offering Texas Hold'em, Omaha and seven-card stud for cash or tournament play.

Enzo slithered across Bill's path, intercepting him before he made it inside. "You're looking sharp as always."

"Good to see you making the rounds," Bill said, swallowing bile as he went through this nightly farce once again.

Given a choice, he'd sooner shove an ice pick in Enzo's heart than spout false pleasantries, but unfortunately, Bill's back was up against the wall and he had to endure this.

For now.

"We need to talk," Enzo said.

"It'll have to wait. I'm busy." Bill let his tone slide toward dismissive.

"Now," Enzo stated coldly, blocking Bill's path. "My office."

Any office was the last place they should talk. Didn't that fool know the radioactive level of scrutiny Bill was under? The FBI had bugs and agents throughout the casino. He'd wager there were federal eyes on them at that very moment. The feds had guys sitting in vans outside his restaurant and house and following him everywhere.

He wouldn't be surprised if whoever the special agent in charge was had a report detailing how often Bill went to the bathroom along with what kind of toilet paper he used.

"Let's have a drink later." Bill patted Enzo on the shoulder. "We'll talk then."

"Full operational control and seventy-five percent of the profits," Enzo said.

Bill chuckled, shoving his hands into his pockets. "I'll see you in hell before I give you seventy-five percent of my casino."

"Not the casino. The girls."

Alarm sent a chill down Bill's spine. Enzo was making a play for the lucrative sex trafficking ring.

"Not here," Bill whispered, glancing around to see if he spotted any of the agents in the vicinity. Between the lounges and displays, casinos were full of loiterers, which made spotting surveillance almost impossible. The feds always had at least two agents tracking him. Sometimes more. Whenever Bill caught one watching him, they quickly looked away.

Did they think avoiding eye contact would make them turn invisible?

It only made them look more suspicious.

A pretty lady with deep olive skin and thick, glossy hair from a Pantene commercial left the Texas Hold'em table and walked their way. She wore a revealing tank top, flashing more skin than a fed would, and slacks. He noted her shoes.

Sensible shoes a person could run in was one telltale of those agents on mobile surveillance.

This woman wore killer high heels and had no qualms meeting Bill's gaze.

"I offered to discuss it in my office. You declined. So we'll do it here," Enzo said, checking out the woman passing by. "I don't care who hears us. It doesn't endanger me. Only you. I don't have a vested interest. Yet." Enzo pulled on a smug grin that Bill wanted to slap off his arrogant face. "The bosses are meeting in a week here in New Orleans to discuss your future."

Time was almost up. Bill needed Edgar and any incriminating information he had on the lot of them pronto. It was his only salvation.

"Look, I'm trying to help you." Enzo's smile widened like he wanted to devour the whole world. "Give them a reason to spare you. After all, we're friends."

"Like a viper and a mongoose are friends," Bill spit. "Which one am I?"

You'll find out when I rip off your damn reptilian

head with my teeth and dance on your cold-blooded corpse. Bill smiled back but said nothing.

Tommy strode over and gave Bill an affirmative nod, which meant one thing.

Devlin had Edgar.

If Bill wasn't standing in the middle of the casino in front of this dirtbag and didn't have bad knees, he would've jumped for joy and pumped his fists in the air. "I'll have something that I think the bosses will be much more interested in," Bill said, "but thanks for the offer."

He'd give the vultures Edgar's bruised and broken body to pick at and use whatever evidence that traitor had squirreled away for old-fashioned blackmail. Put them back in their places. Show 'em Big Bill was the boss once again ruling New Orleans.

"It better be good or it's your funeral." Enzo turned and left.

Bill took a cleansing breath and led his nephew to one of the four restaurants in the casino. They entered the busy, gleaming kitchen. He acknowledged the head chef and some of the underlings and went into the walk-in refrigerator, where sides of beef hung from the ceiling. Tommy closed the door behind him.

It was freezing in the tin icebox, but it was a safe space to talk freely.

"What did Enzo want?" Tommy asked.

"Seventy-five percent of the sex ring."

"Wow." Tommy rocked back on his heels. "They're really gunning for you."

Didn't Bill know it. But it was time for him to hit back. "Don't worry about it. I've got a plan."

"No offense, but I gotta worry." Tommy's breath

fogged the cold air. "If they slit your throat, Uncle Bill, I'm going to bleed out with you."

The kid's concern was warranted, and Bill had an obligation to protect his sister's only son. "You spoke to Devlin?"

Tommy nodded, rubbing his hands together. "D got him. *Alive.* The boys just passed through Tucson. They'll reach the city in twenty-one hours, but D is flying back tomorrow. He got delayed in San Diego. When he gets back, he wants to meet face-to-face."

"You told him we'll do it at Avido's?" The casino wasn't an option and Bill's days of meeting in back alleys and cars were done. He was reduced to having conversations in meat lockers, for Pete's sake.

"Yeah. I told him," Tommy said. "He wants to arrange half the payment before his boys set foot in New Orleans with Edgar. The rest on delivery."

Bill blew into his cupped hands, starting to shiver. "Fine. Whatever he wants. As long as I get Edgar alive. And what about the evidence? Digital? Hard copies? Anything?"

Tommy shrugged. "D said he's working on it."

"What the hell is that supposed to mean?"

"He said he'd explain in person."

Bill was too damn cold to blow a fuse.

Nabbing Edgar was a major win. Bill would toss the other bosses a juicy Plinski bone to gnaw on, but he needed that evidence—in black and white, so to speak—to get out of this alive.

SOMETIMES ASSISTANT SPECIAL AGENT in Charge Ava Garcia strolled through the casino on one of her breaks or after duty, to play a hand of poker or have a meal.

She liked to change her shoes first. A woman walked differently depending on her footwear. Three-inch heels didn't scream federal agent but purred all-woman.

It helped her blend in, appear nonthreatening.

Garcia spent more time at the Windfall than she did at her apartment in the hopes she'd see something, overhear a nugget she could use to nail Big Bill Walsh to the wall.

Today she'd got that kernel, making all her free hours spent here worthwhile.

The other bosses in the syndicate were coming to New Orleans. That was huge.

Bill would have to meet with them, and he planned to offer them something they wanted more than his head on a pike.

She'd have to get extra agents and change out the vehicles Bill's people were familiar with. Anticipate how Big Bill would try to give them the slip.

No matter what, the FBI would also be in attendance.

Garcia watched Bill and his nephew leave the restaurant. They were rubbing their arms, looking chilled to the bone.

What were you two talking about in a meat locker?

Garcia left the casino, headed to her car in the parking garage and called her boss, Special Agent in Charge Bryan McCaffrey. "Sir, Garcia here. I'm going to need four more agents and to swap out vehicles as soon as possible."

AIDEN FOLLOWED THE directions Charlie gave him as she finished eating her burger.

Twenty minutes later, he turned off the highway and pulled into the cracked parking lot of the Oasis. Red

*X*s blazed with the promise of scantily clad adult entertainment.

"Why on earth are we at a strip club and how is it going to solve any of our problems?" Aiden usually trusted Charlie without question, but he looked at her like she was crazy.

"If I tell you, you won't like it."

"You're not going in there to strip, are you?" As soon as the words left his mouth, he regretted it, hearing how absurd it sounded. They didn't need money, but they were here for some unfathomable reason.

"Of course not. How is stripping going to help us?"

He threw his hands in the air and shrugged.

"Sit tight," she said, patting his leg. "I'll be back as soon as I can. Thirty minutes, tops."

Before he could protest about how this was a bad idea, whatever she was up to, Charlie was out of the truck and sauntering inside the Oasis.

Aiden left the vehicle running. No telling what Charlie was doing in there. Best for him to stay prepared for anything.

There were twelve cars in the lot on a Friday at three o'clock in the afternoon. Might be a payday for some.

A shame to blow it here. Then again, the women inside had to make a living, too.

Aiden stared at the red pulsing *X*s. An unspecified anxiety twisted through him. His thoughts raced.

Why couldn't he go inside with her? It was a gentlemen's club, after all. Why wouldn't he like her plan? Did it involve some dude rubbing his hands all over her?

"This is stupid," he muttered to himself. "I'll just go in there and see for myself."

No sooner had he cut the engine and taken out the

key than Charlie came out, looking pleased as a cat that'd swallowed a canary.

She jumped in as he started the truck.

"Drive," she said.

He threw the truck in gear and turned onto the highway. "Talk. Now."

"Ta-da," she said, pulling two driver's licenses and a credit card out of her back pocket and holding them up next to each other. "You are now Rudy Benally and I'm Priscilla Johnson."

Aiden took one. Arizona State driver's license. The guy was forty, eight years older than Aiden, Native American, short black hair. Height five-ten, off by only two inches. Weight 180, lighter by twenty. But they didn't look enough alike to even appear related.

"Sorry I couldn't do better with yours. There were only two Native American guys inside to choose from."

Taking a glance at the other, he noticed a resemblance between Charlie and Priscilla. Blond hair. Blue eyes. Twenty-seven. Four years younger than Charlie. But time hadn't been kind and the woman in the photo looked older. Same height and weight. Priscilla was pretty while Charlie was gorgeous.

The credit card was in Priscilla's name.

"With your baseball cap," Charlie said, "this will work."

He gritted his teeth, not liking it, but he didn't have a better plan. "Did you pick-pocket all of that? As soon as the credit card is reported stolen, we're hosed."

"Ms. Johnson works there. She's a shrewd, resourceful businesswoman who was open to making a deal. I paid her to loan me her license and credit card. There's a thousand-dollar limit on the credit, so I gave her fifteen hundred, with the promise that I'd mail both back to her. For an extra two hundred, she was kind enough to help me separate Mr. Benally, a touchy-feely jerk and bad tipper, from his license. If it makes you happy, we can mail that back, too, since we have his address."

He heaved a big sigh. "Fine. We'll give it a go. But since we can't fly with firearms, we need to secure them."

"How far to Phoenix?"

"Two, maybe three hours," he said, tracking her thinking. Nick was there visiting Lori. They could park the truck at the airport and let him know where to pick it up. They'd also have more options of flights from the larger hub. "Phoenix it is."

Aiden took I-8 to I-10. Traffic in and out of a large city was always dicey, but with them only stopping once to use the restroom, they made great time.

At the Sky Harbor International Airport, they parked at the terminal and stowed their vests and firearms under a seat in the truck but hung on to their badges and comms devices.

Charlie also kept the gym bag.

"What else is in there?" Aiden asked.

"The supplies to stitch up your arm. They won't let us through security with everything, so I'll check the bag."

"Thanks," he said. "For thinking about it." That was what they did, took care of each other.

"No problem." She grabbed what was left of her soda and held it up. "In case we need a diversion when they check our IDs."

He locked the doors, placing the fob back in the key box, and had Charlie make sure no one was watching while he put it back under the carriage.

They walked directly to ticketing and checked the departure boards. A Delta flight to Baton Rouge. Ninety-minute drive. But it was boarding now. United had one leaving in forty minutes to New Orleans. A nonstop flight.

"Let's hope they have tickets," Aiden said.

The line at the ticket counter was short and moved quickly. A weary-looking woman of about sixty greeted them when it was their turn.

"We're hoping to get two seats on your last flight to New Orleans." Charlie placed the soda cup with plastic lid on the counter.

The woman clicked away on her keyboard. "I have a handful left. None together, unfortunately. But you'll have to hurry to make it."

"Sounds good," Aiden said, setting down Benally's license. "One bag to check."

"Thanks so much." Charlie handed over the ID and credit card. "He just got a big promotion and I promised we'd go there to celebrate. My treat."

The woman lined the identification up in front of her and typed in their information, glancing between the cards and the screen, disinterested in their story, but Charlie kept talking.

"You've worked so hard. You deserve to have some fun." She wrapped her arm around his and put her head on his shoulder.

"*We* deserve some fun," he said, playing along as if they were a couple.

The woman swiped the credit card and took the bag. She typed some more, and the machine printed boarding cards. After attaching the baggage tag to their one checked item, she collated the tickets with the right licenses. "You two better hurry. Enjoy your trip and congratulations on your promotion," she said, handing them over.

Charlie picked up her soda with a smile. "Have a good evening."

They jogged to the checkpoint, where it was one person's sole job to verify a picture ID against the ticket. They got in place with the string of passengers and shuffled forward.

Loosening the plastic lid on her cup, Charlie adjusted it to sit on top instead of clicked down in place. Aiden lowered the bill of his cap.

Next in line, they were waved forward.

Charlie took his ticket and license, slipping them behind hers. They stepped up to the podium together, and she handed over everything to the fortysomething screener.

The man looked down at Priscilla's license and up at Charlie. Appearing satisfied, he scribbled a mark on the ticket and gave Charlie back hers.

Then the screener glanced at Benally's license.

As the middle-aged man's gaze lifted to Aiden, Charlie stepped to the side and tripped.

The lid of her cup flew off. Soda splashed on the floor, drawing everyone's attention.

"Darn it," she said. "I'm sorry about the mess. I really wanted to finish that, too."

"It's all right, miss. We'll get it cleaned up. You were going to have to toss that anyway before you got through security." He scribbled on Aiden's ticket and handed it to him along with the license and then gestured for them to move on. "Watch your step, please."

Clearing the rest of security was a breeze. They put

their badges discreetly in the plastic tray along with their communication devices, the flash drive, shoes and the cell phone.

If they had been traveling on official business, they would have had their sidearms, gone to the head of the line and then through a side door.

As regular joes, they each took a turn in the security hoop, hands raised, boots off.

On the other side, they finished lacing up their boots and headed to the gate. It was fairly empty. The majority of passengers taking the flight had already boarded.

"Where are you seated?" she asked.

"Row twenty-three. Aisle. You?"

"Ten. Window. I'll talk to a flight attendant and see if she can get someone to switch."

The cell phone rang. Aiden took it out. "Nick's number."

"Good thing he called before we got on."

Their plane was going to land late in the Louis Armstrong Airport, after eleven.

He hit the answer button. "It's Aiden."

"Hey, man. I wish I was calling with better news."

Aiden met Charlie's gaze and shook his head. "Give me a sec." He took her elbow and steered her off into a corner, out of anyone else's earshot, and put the call on speaker. "Go ahead. We can both hear you."

Charlie paced in front of him, her hands on her hips.

"I've got details about the eyewitness," Nick said. "He was supposedly hiking at Mission Trail Park. As he was leaving, going south on Mission Gorge Road, headed back to a friend's house, where he was staying while on vacation, he claims he saw Yazzie shoot Torres and Killinger take out the cop."

"Vacation?" Aiden asked. "If he's not from San Diego, where does he live?"

"New Orleans," Nick said.

That jarred Charlie to a stop. "Are you kidding me?"

"Albatross is from New Orleans. You said yourself he has a powerful enemy there, a mobster who wants him dead," Aiden said. "Doesn't anyone find that the least bit suspicious?"

"The man has half a dozen powerful enemies from Houston to Biloxi. The eyewitness's friend, his reason for being in San Diego, checks out, and the time of his 911 call fits the time of the incident. So far his story is so airtight it can't breathe."

Charlie muttered a curse. "Albatross said the person who had the biggest ax to grind with him was a guy back home."

"Do you have proof? Or is it just hearsay? Speculation?" Nick sighed. "Listen, no one is going to take your word. Everyone believes the eyewitness lock, stock and barrel," Nick said with grim resignation. "From the police chief to Draper, who, by the way, has thrown you two to the wolves. It doesn't look good. The witness is hanging around San Diego for any follow-up questions and plans to leave tomorrow, seven p.m. flight back to New Orleans."

"What about the dead cop's body-worn camera?" Aiden asked.

"The BWC was no help. There was too much smoke and his car door obstructed most of the video. The audio does nothing to clear you. I'm sorry the news isn't better, but I'm rooting for you guys."

"We're being set up," Charlie said. "Why is everyone so quick to dismiss our track record and believe this witness? What is he? A priest?"

"No. He's a cop."

Cold sweat broke out on Aiden's back. "Are you sure?"

"Yep. His police chief in the Fifth District attested to his honesty, integrity and astounding service record in SWAT."

The truth closed in on him. The fluidity of the men who had attacked them. Their precision. Their paramilitary approach. Their...*professionalism.*

They'd been ambushed by a special weapons and tactics team.

"This just keeps getting better and better," Charlie said.

"Do you have a name and address?" Aiden asked.

"Sure do. His name is Frank Devlin."

Chapter Ten

Everything Nick had told them played on a loop in Charlie's head during the three-hour flight. She and Aiden had to go up against a corrupt SWAT team.

Without backup.

Without weapons.

On the enemy's turf.

She cursed the hand they'd been dealt.

A flight attendant had managed to get Charlie and Aiden seats together, but they hadn't been able to risk discussing their predicament on the flight.

Her skin itched, and she couldn't wait to get off the aircraft and move.

The plane's touchdown was smooth and the taxi to the terminal was fast. The tiny chime sounded, the seatbelt light went out, and passengers leaped to their feet to disembark.

The plane emptied from the front, people moving in a steady single-file stream, funneling out row by row. Charlie and Aiden went out the door onto the Jetway. Muggy air and the stench of kerosene hit them, and they moved on into the Louis Armstrong Airport.

Thanks to their flight time plus the two-hour timezone change, it was eleven thirty.

Nick had passed along Devlin's address. That was where they'd start.

They had to find the place on Rampart Street in the Seventh Ward, break in and search the dirty cop's home for anything that might help them.

Sounded simple enough, but in the pit of her stomach she knew better.

They went to the taxi line and slipped into the back seat of a sedan. Not as if they could take a cab to the cop's house.

"We need a car rental company," Aiden said.

"Which one?" the driver asked. "Enterprise? Avis?"

"No, none of those." Charlie shook her head. "Not one of the big brands or anything in the yellow pages. We want something away from the airport. Small. Discreet."

The driver flashed a lopsided grin. "I know just the spot."

Without asking questions, he drove them to a place fifteen minutes away. A lot with about twenty cars, located next to an auto salvage yard. There was a little shack situated between both properties, with two signs—Dan's Auto Wreckage and Dealing Dan's Car Rentals.

The driver honked twice.

A minute later, the door of the shack opened, and a man wearing a fedora stuck his head out and waved.

"You're good to go," the driver said.

Aiden peeled off a couple of twenties and took care of the cab fare, and then they walked to the shack.

"Looking to rent a car?" the older guy asked them.

Aiden nodded. "Yeah. Something with a navigation system. We don't know the city."

"Take a look at the five cars in the first row. Those have GPS. When you find something you like, give a holler. I'm Dealing Dan." He tipped his fedora to them and then disappeared back inside like he could've just as easily been called Shady Dan.

Bypassing the BMW and Mercedes-Benz, they looked at the Toyota, Honda and Chevy Impala. They needed something fast that would blend in and not call attention to them regardless of the neighborhood they might find themselves in.

"The Honda is out," Aiden said. "Too many scratches and dents."

"I don't like that bright cherry-apple red color of the Toyota," Charlie said. Too memorable when they wanted to be utterly forgettable.

Aiden agreed. "I guess we have a winner."

They walked to the shack and knocked on the door.

"Come on in." A comedy show played on a television behind the desk, where Dan had his feet up and hands resting on his big belly. "What'd you decide on?"

"The black Impala," Aiden said. "Is it reliable?"

"As reliable as it's going to get," Dan said, chuckling at the screen. "It's a 2005, one hundred and fifty thousand miles, new timing belt and tires. Runs smooth. Shouldn't give you any problems. How long will you need it?"

Aiden and Charlie exchanged a glance, an unspoken question passing between them. How long did Albatross have to live?

"Three days," Aiden said.

"At the most," Charlie added.

They did the deal using the licenses of Johnson and Benally, and Johnson's credit card. Charlie filled out the paperwork, listing a fake phone number and bogus address. So long as Dealing Dan got paid, Charlie suspected he wouldn't care too much if the information was made up.

Dan handed over the key. "Be sure to get some beignets from Café du Monde while you're here and try the coffee with chicory. Nothing else quite like it. Enjoy your time in New Orleans."

"One more thing," Charlie said. "Would it be safe to assume with you working out here at all hours by yourself that you're packing?"

Dan smiled. "Yeah, it would."

"Willing to sell us your gun?" she asked.

"No can do. But I can offer some nonlethal options." Dealing Dan pulled out a baseball bat and a crowbar and set them on the desk.

Neither were inconspicuous options, but they'd work under the cover of darkness.

"We'll take both," Aiden said.

At a significant upcharge, one hundred dollars bought them two weapons.

They climbed into the Chevy. The tints on the windows were a bit chipped and starting to bubble and the sagging seats creaked when they sat on them, but the engine turned over with no drama.

The address on Rampart Street was easy to find with the navigation system. The neighborhood had a bohemian vibe, colorful street murals, quirky boutiques and hip-looking restaurants.

Devlin's place was a small shotgun row house on a residential street with a driveway alongside. They parked two doors down across the street.

Charlie dug out two sets of plastic gloves from the

box she'd taken from the hospital and handed some to Aiden. "So we don't leave any prints."

Putting them on, he said, "You really do have quite the criminal mind."

"What can I say? I'm a product of my environment."

"It's been useful." He put a hand on her shoulder and squeezed, filling her with warmth.

For the first time in her life, she wasn't ashamed or embarrassed about growing up in foster care and group homes. Even though Aiden had had a picture-perfect home with a loving mother and devoted father, he had a way of seeing her, accepting her, that made her feel valued and special.

They got out of the car, carrying their overpriced weapons, and crept around the long, narrow home. Red security storm doors were on the front and back, where there was also a small patio.

"Please tell me you learned how to pick a lock, too," Aiden said.

Charlie shrugged. "I did, but it's not like I have the right tools on me. We should try a window."

They did, but they were all locked.

"I'll have to break a windowpane," Aiden said.

That was when she noticed the aluminum sill. It was easily breakable. "No. Too risky. Someone could hear the glass breaking. I think I can jimmy it open."

She shoved the flat edge of the crowbar between the window and the sill. As she leveraged the pane up, Aiden pushed. The sash latch gave way and the window slid open.

He gave her a boost, with her foot on his palms, and she hoisted herself up the frame and climbed inside. Aiden followed behind her and they closed the window.

The houses on the street had historic charm on the outside, but inside, this one had been renovated with high-end finishes and stainless-steel appliances.

It was a straightforward two-bedroom, two-and-a-half-bath home. The living room flowed into the dining room and on to the kitchen.

They split up and searched the place. Aiden took the master bedroom and the other one set up as an office/guest room.

Charlie started in the kitchen. There was nothing hidden in the fridge or freezer. No false backs in the cupboards, no fake tins of coffee, nothing hidden in the jars of flour or sugar. No voids behind the wallboards.

Next, she checked the dining room and living room. No loose boards in the hardwood floor, no hollowed-out books. Nothing in the sofa cushions, either.

She blew out a frustrated breath and spun around to see what she might've missed.

On the wall in the dining room hung some pictures. Most of the photos were of one man surrounded by nature. *Frank Devlin.*

He knew their faces and names and now they knew his, too.

Early to midforties. Six-two. Athletic build. Rugged. A thick head of sandy brown hair. Eyes so intense they were chilling.

In one photo, Devlin held up a huge fish by a lake. Another was of him kneeling beside a dead deer in a meadow covered in mist. Two teenagers stood in front of a cabin in the next one. A boy with his arm around a younger girl's shoulders. They resembled one another. Brother and sister.

She stared at the last picture. Five men, smiling,

standing together behind a bar. A backlit sign read The Merry Men.

Robin Hood's band of outlaws. Mighty brazen of them.

"I've got nothing," Aiden said, walking out of the office. "Not even a laptop. Any luck?"

"I think this is Devlin." She pulled out the cell phone and took a picture of the photo with the men. They looked like standard-issue tough guys: hardened, brawny, merciless beneath the smiles. Badges and guns on their hips. Devlin had his right hand on the shoulder of the man in the middle. "There's five of them here. But we were hit by a team of four. What if one of them stayed behind?"

"Only one way to find out. Are you up for a drink?"

"Always."

A 411 CALL GOT them the address. The parking lot of The Merry Men was almost full. Only a few spots left at the far end by a wall. The idea of getting blocked in didn't sit well with Aiden.

He parked across the street. "Stay here and keep it running."

"Come again?"

"One or more cops own that bar. That'll make it a *cop bar.*"

She turned in her seat and faced him. "And?"

"Bars are already a weapons-rich environment with glasses, longneck beer bottles, even heavier wine bottles." You could club a person with one. "If they have pool tables, that'll mean pool cues."

Charlie's brow furrowed. "I have been in a bar. I'm familiar."

"But in *that* bar, most of the patrons are going to be packing heat, and we can't stroll in with a crowbar and baseball bat. We need answers about a dirty cop. Answers no one inside is going to willingly give. If the car is running, it'll be easier to make a quick getaway if push comes to shove."

Her frown deepened. "Why am I supposed to be the one left in the car? And if you give me 'it's an order' or 'I outrank you' crap, I think we'll have to arm wrestle for it."

He suppressed a chuckle. "I can take you in an arm wrestle."

"Not the way I play."

Which meant no rules. Winning by any means necessary.

Would she throw a fist to his groin?

"Follow the order without giving me grief," he said, wanting to avoid an arm wrestle. "We can debate it later." If it came down to a fistfight, he'd rather be the only one getting his butt kicked. Spare her a beatdown from a bunch of cops.

"I have a better idea."

"Really?" He raised a suspicious brow. "What's that?"

She took off her jacket, tucked her short sleeves up into the body of her T-shirt, displaying her toned arms, and pulled the V-neck front down, showing off her ample cleavage.

He realized how she intended to play this, and it made his gut churn with a shocking possessiveness.

"You keep the car running while I drop a little bait and separate our prey from the herd." She fluffed her hair. "I'd kill for lipstick and a little mascara."

Aiden gritted his teeth, hating her impetuous plan from start to finish. "You look better without it," he said without thinking. "Prettier."

Charlie's gaze flew to his as her jaw dropped a little.

He usually kept such comments to himself, not wanting to make her uncomfortable by reminding her that he saw her as an enticing woman.

Since he'd started speaking his mind, why stop there?

"You're a natural beauty, Charlie." He dared run his knuckle along the side of her face. "You'll have every guy in there drooling, wishing he could take you home tonight."

A slight flush stained her cheeks, and she gulped.

Maybe he'd been playing it too safe, not telling her, not showing her how much he desired her. Waiting for her to be ready. Sometimes a person had to be thrown into a sink-or-swim position.

He lowered his hand, cupping her neck. Her pulse throbbed against his palm. "Do me a favor and stay here. Don't make me watch you smile and flirt with some guy while he ogles you. Touches you." If he had to choose between that and a potential fistfight, bring on the brawl.

She wet her lips and clutched his wrist but didn't pull his hand away, turning him on bright as a bulb. Her eyes were luminous. Radiant with a hunger, a fire that drew him closer even though he knew he'd get burned.

The atmosphere in the car shifted, like the current in the air before a storm.

Her mouth opened, but before she could speak, he followed a foreign, reckless impulse and leaned over, pressing his lips to hers.

There was none of the cautious gentleness of a first

kiss. No need to coax. No resistance given. All the desire that'd been kindling for four years ignited in hot bliss.

It was a long-overdue communion that touched him to the very core.

She arched up and let him in. As he sank into her warm mouth, his hand slid up, cupping the back of her head. He devoured her, slowly, deeply, consuming and claiming. Every slick swipe of her tongue against his was liquid heat.

Holding her to him, he deepened the kiss as he found himself pushing her back in the seat.

A headiness enveloped him, seeping to every nerve fiber, but he forced himself to stop.

He pulled back, not wanting to ever let her go.

Her eyes fluttered open and he saw it—the evasiveness of her gaze, the set of her mouth, the stiffening of her posture, the crease in her brow. He'd cataloged every nuance of her body language, memorized every elusive emotion that passed across her face. She was retreating behind her wall.

His heart squeezed.

"If you don't want to watch, you should stay here and keep the car running." She hopped out, slammed the door and started crossing the street.

Aiden cut the engine and was hot on her heels. "Charlie!"

"What's the alternative? You get your face busted up, maybe a few broken ribs. No. Not on my watch." Stepping onto the sidewalk, she turned and faced him. "We should go in separately. If he's in there, I'll get him outside around back." Then she opened the door and disappeared inside.

Aiden scrubbed a hand over his face, hauling in a deep breath. That kiss. God, *that kiss* had been all-consuming. Set him ablaze, painting everything with a pall of red.

There was something he'd learned today, a lesson that had to be heeded.

Life could turn on a dime. His reputation and career hung in the balance. Circumstances kept shifting like grains of sand beneath their feet.

His love for Charlie was the one constant. In fact, it had got stronger since his tumble off the roof. Brought everything into high definition and surround sound.

He was done avoiding, making excuses, playing it safe. No more holding himself back.

SOG. Camp Beauregard. He had to tell her.

The secret he was keeping from her about the job offer was eating him up. The deadline to give an answer was next Friday. Eons away in light of what they were currently facing—

Finding Edgar and clearing their names.

Next Friday, he could be sitting in a jail cell, trying to explain how things had gone terribly wrong—or worse. And his biggest regret would be not telling Charlie how he felt about her.

He shoved the darkest thoughts from his mind. They'd get through this the way they did every other mission. As a team.

Aiden adjusted his ball cap and went into the bar.

It was wood-paneled, with taxidermied heads of deer, bobcats and gators protruding from the walls, and had a long line of taps that would've been a beer lover's dream come true. All the tables and booths were taken.

He grabbed the first seat he found near the door. Next

to him was a tall guy, thin as a blade but wiry, with a gun and badge on his hip. Taking stock of his surroundings, Aiden counted ten more badges and guns in ten seconds. He spotted Charlie perched on a stool at the opposite end of the bar.

The guy from the picture, the one who'd been in the middle, was behind the bar, pouring her a drink and chatting her up. She sucked back the clear liquid in the shot glass and set it down.

The man poured her and himself another round. They clinked glasses and did the shot.

She worked fast.

Color Aiden unsurprised.

Not much of a beer drinker, he ordered a double bourbon, neat. A female bartender didn't waste time getting his order and was heavy-handed with the pour.

Aiden dropped a twenty on the bar. "Is that the owner?" He gestured to Mr. McChatty.

"*One* of the owners. Jeff Landau."

"How many others?"

She pointed to a picture hanging on the wall. The same as the one at Devlin's place. "Four. But Jeff is the only one here right now."

"Where are the rest?"

She shrugged. "Vacation. Hunting trip, I think."

"They all active over at the Fifth District?"

"Yeah, except Jeff. He retired a couple of years ago."

The dude sitting beside him gave Aiden the side-eye. *One too many questions asked. Got it.* "Thanks," he said to the waitress and grabbed a handful of nuts from a bowl.

Watching the crowd through the mirror behind the

bar, he estimated 75 percent of the patrons, including the man next to him, were cops. Either active or retired.

He nursed his bourbon while Charlie flirted and laughed and slammed back shots, throwing out stellar bait only a eunuch could resist.

A strange possessiveness roared through him. He'd never wanted any woman the way he wanted Charlie. In his bed, beneath him, above him, curled around him. In his life, beside him.

He put his jealousy in check as he'd done many times before, but the ache in his chest didn't go away. He'd dared showing her his feelings, asked her not to do this, and she'd done it anyway.

Charlie took another shot. He wasn't worried about her holding her liquor. She was able to drink a Russian under the table with his own vodka. He just didn't want to watch her throw herself at another man, even if it was playing a role.

In thirty grueling minutes, she had McChatty hooked.

Charlie stood, leaned over the bar, arching her back, projecting her breasts, her tight, round butt high in the air, and whispered in Jeff's ear.

The massive ball of tension inside Aiden burned hotter than a solar flare.

Every man in the vicinity checked her out, lust stamped on their faces, gleaming in their eyes. They were practically drooling. Aiden couldn't blame them. With no makeup, wearing jeans and a T-shirt, Charlie was stunning. Truly something to behold.

Jeff spoke to the other bartender for a second, and she responded with a nod and a sly smile. Then he led Charlie through a door outside to the back.

His muscles tightened, but he resisted the urge to

jump up and leave right away. With his hand clenched in a fist on his thigh, he finished his drink. When the stopwatch in his head hit two minutes, he spun off his stool, yawned for good measure and went out the front.

As soon as the door closed, he forced himself to walk slow and easy, like time wasn't a factor, with his hands in his pockets, around the side of the building toward the back. A man running, especially one of color, drew unwanted attention and suspicion faster than one strolling along without a care in the world.

By the time he made his way to the dumpster, Charlie had Jeff pinned with his cheek pressed to the brick wall, his arm twisted behind his back at an angle meant to cause excruciating pain, with his pants down around his ankles.

From the blood on his face, she'd broken his nose first.

"Devlin and the others, who hired them?" she asked as Aiden came up alongside her.

"I don't know what you're talking about."

"She's got quite a temper," Aiden said, "and she's short on patience. I suggest you start talking."

"You're both making a big mistake. Messing with the wrong people."

Charlie gestured for Aiden to take over holding Jeff. He was more than happy to oblige.

After they swapped places, she snatched his right wrist and twisted until the knuckles were facing her. She grabbed his index finger. "The job in San Diego. Who hired him?"

Jeff called Charlie a bunch of foul names. In Aiden's experience, she wasn't going to respond well.

Without a word, she wrenched his finger back ninety degrees, snapping the first knuckle.

Jeff gasped and groaned in sheer shock and pain.

Impressive. He took it like a champ, without screaming.

"I tried to warn you," Aiden said.

"Tell us who or I break another and another until you won't be able to pour drinks with that hand, and then I'll move on to the other."

"Big Bill," he grunted.

They exchanged a glance. "Yeah, we're not from around here," Aiden said. "We're going to need a last name."

"Walsh. Big Bill Walsh."

"Why didn't you go with your buddies?" she asked.

"I busted my knee a couple of years ago. Forced retirement. I'm no good to them anymore out there like this."

"Why was Devlin hired for the job?"

She grabbed his middle finger when Jeff didn't immediately answer her question.

"Because Big Bill wants Edgar Plinski. The guy's a rat who killed his sister."

Aiden hadn't seen that coming. Most in WITSEC were some brand of criminal, but Edgar didn't seem the murdering kind. The Department of Justice was certainly unaware of the allegation. If it was true, he'd be out of the program, since the immunity deal that he'd been given didn't cover murder.

"Why is Big Bill offering so much money for any information Plinski might have in his possession?" Charlie asked, on a roll.

"Big Bill needs it. The other bosses are slowly squeezing him out. Enzo Romero already took half of his casino. It's only a matter of time before he ends up floating in the river. No fingertips. No dental records. That's if the FBI who've got him under surveillance don't arrest him first."

"Which casino?" Aiden asked.

"Which?" Jeff made it sound as if the answer should've been obvious. "The only real one in the city. Windfall."

"Hey!" someone called from the street. "What are you doing? Jeff? Is that you?"

"Time to go," Aiden said to Charlie.

Shots rang out as they took off down the alley.

Chapter Eleven

A second shot was fired somewhere behind them.

They rounded the corner, sprinted down the pavement and took another right turn, running side by side.

At the car, Aiden slid in behind the steering wheel and fired up the engine as Charlie dropped into the passenger seat. Without waiting for her to close the door, he swerved into traffic and peeled off down the street.

Pure adrenaline pumped in her blood and her head buzzed, but her thoughts circled around one thing.

Aiden Yazzie kissed me! Something she'd longed for and dreaded all at once.

And she had kissed him back. Without thinking, without choosing. It had been as necessary as breathing, and stopping hadn't even been a whisper in her head.

His sexy mouth, his hot tongue… When they'd touched hers, everything had trembled. Her lips, her limbs, her bones, her heart. She would've sworn that the car had shaken.

He'd kissed her so deeply that she couldn't tell where he ended and she began. She'd forgotten the rules, the boundaries, her name.

It was a good thing they'd been in a car parked on a city street. If they'd been anywhere remotely private, there would've been no stopping. The tension and touching would've grown hot and feverish, turning volcanic, until they were both ready to explode, their bodies demanding a release.

Arousing, erotic, enthrallingly rough images flooded her mind.

Crap. What the hell did this mean?

Did she really want to know?

Nope. Then she'd have to deal with it, which meant making a mess of things. Better to pretend it had never happened. Though it had, and she'd never forget it for as long as she lived.

"What's up?" Aiden asked.

"Huh?"

"You were shaking your head and then you were nodding at something."

"Oh, was I?" She cleared her throat, struggling for composure. "I was just thinking about bed. For sex. I mean sleep. For sleeping," she said again, emphasizing the word with her hand. "It's been a long day. I'm so exhausted that I'm delirious. I don't know what I'm saying. We need to find a hotel."

"Okay." He gave her a weird look. "Should be easy enough."

They chose a hotel on the outskirts of the French Quarter. A large, busy place with a heavy flow of tourists, but not surrounded by too much noise.

It was within walking distance of restaurants, shops of all kind and the Windfall Casino.

They parked in the hotel's garage. Aiden carried their one bag.

Walking up to the check-in desk, she realized they

didn't have basic toiletries. Or pajamas. They'd have to sleep naked in the same room.

A hot rush of panic shot through her, stilling her.

Aiden's hand went to the small of her back and he ushered her forward.

The clerk welcomed them with a smile. "Good evening."

"We'd like to get a room," Aiden said.

"How many nights?"

Aiden looked at her and she shrugged. Edgar had been gone almost twelve hours. He had another sixty to live, tops, if he was lucky.

"Two nights," Aiden said. "A room away from the ice machine and near the stairs."

They didn't need the noise of the machine, or a reason for anyone to loiter near their room, and it was always good to be close to a second exit.

Charlie set the borrowed credit card on the counter.

"I'd prefer to leave cash to cover any incidentals," Aiden said, surprising her at first.

On the chance Priscilla Johnson decided to report it stolen, order a new one and keep the fifteen hundred without worrying about the bill, it could put them in an awkward situation. Not to mention it'd give the hotel a reason to call the police.

Cash was best.

"No problem," the clerk said. "For cash, we require two hundred and fifty dollars to cover any phone calls, the minibar and pay-per-view charges. If you order room service, you'll have to pay the waitstaff when they deliver it."

Aiden dug out enough bills from his wad of hundreds

to cover the two-night stay plus incidentals. In return, the clerk handed them two key cards.

They swung by the mini-mart in the lobby, grabbed toiletries and got in the elevator.

She only meant to give Aiden's reflection in the shiny steel wall a quick glance, but her eyes lingered. On his strong jaw. His dark T-shirt stretched tight across his shoulders. His hard muscles. Those legs that looked incredible in a pair of shorts, sexier filling out jeans. Probably best with nothing on at all.

And man, he could kiss. She had wanted to lose herself in the confident, demanding way he'd owned her mouth with so much passion, melting her protective barrier of ice into a puddle of desire. If that was how he kissed, how did he do other things?

A sensation she couldn't name exploded through her. Stronger than lust. Animalistic and primitive. And she needed to shake it off quick.

With a ding, the elevator stopped, and the doors opened to the fourth floor. They found their room at the end of the hall. He opened the door, letting her in ahead of him.

She entered, taking in the spacious room, and froze.

There was one king-size bed.

"I can go change the room to a double," Aiden said.

Always the gentleman, never wanting to put her in a compromising position that other men would've orchestrated.

Deep down, she didn't know what she wanted. She'd fantasized about making love with Aiden more times than she could count on her fingers and toes combined. They were as close as two people could be without sleeping together. But in her experience, sex had a way of spoiling things. She'd do anything not to ruin their relationship.

Aiden was the only good thing in her life.

"Don't worry about it," she said. "I still have to stitch you up and it's almost three in the morning." They were both grown-ups and could handle sharing a bed.

Naked?

Maybe they'd have to sleep in their clothes.

"Why don't you shower first," Aiden said, and she nodded.

In the bathroom, she was relieved to find plush robes and slippers. The velvet-soft cotton would be much nicer to sleep in than her jeans.

Aiden knocked on the door. "Do you want me to order room service?"

I have one hell of an appetite. "No. I'm fine." She was starving, but it was her growing hunger for him that worried her. The last thing they needed was to lounge on the bed in robes, with nothing on beneath, eating and talking, having a drink from the minibar. It was a recipe for trouble. Hot, sweaty, naked trouble. "I'd rather hit the hay sooner, wake up earlier and have a monster-sized breakfast, if that's okay with you."

He didn't respond right away. Then he said, "All right."

She brushed her teeth and hurried through her shower, washing her hair. After towel-drying, she threw on her robe, tying the belt in a knot to prevent any mishaps, and went into the bedroom. She avoided eye contact with him and headed for the bag sitting on the dresser.

"Bathroom is all yours. As soon as you're done, I'll stitch you up and then we can go to *sleep*," she said, enunciating the last word slowly.

Although sex, not sleep, was at the forefront of her mind and her sensitive spots were in cahoots, ready for action. Ridiculous hormones.

It didn't help that she hadn't had sex in more months than she'd cared to admit.

"Sure," he said. The bathroom door shut behind him.

She relaxed, taking a breath.

On the other side of the TV, she noticed two empty protein shake containers. He must've gone back down to the mini-mart because he was starving, too.

Way to go, Killinger. Could you be any more selfish or paranoid?

She rummaged in the bag, took out the supplies, setting up on the desk beside a bright lamp, and put on latex gloves.

Aiden emerged from the bathroom. He stood in the doorway with a towel wrapped around his waist and another in his hand as he dried his hair, looking annoyingly delicious.

Her throat went bone-dry.

He crossed the room, shoved the chair out of the way and sat on the edge of the desk.

This wasn't the first time she'd seen his broad, muscled chest, those nicely formed pecs and washboard abs *completely bare*, but it was the first time she'd been close enough to stick her tongue out and lick every toned, sculpted muscle.

Perfection.

He was striking, had a sparkling energy that was warm, powerful, sexual. A magnetic presence that drew lesser objects into the heat of his sun.

Three minutes after they met and talked one-on-one,

she would've dropped her panties for him, but he'd had a girlfriend at the time.

A saving grace that had allowed their friendship to blossom, given them a chance to become family. But looking at him now, butterflies fluttered in her belly. She had to squeeze her knees together to keep from spreading her legs apart.

She grabbed saline solution and the towel from his hand to catch the runoff. "Ready?"

Aiden gave a curt nod.

This was going to hurt him, and she hated that, but there was no way around it. Had to be done. She squeezed the saline into the wound to irrigate it and rinse off the last of the hemostatic powder.

When the liquid hit his skin, he gave a sharp hiss through gritted teeth.

"Sorry about that."

The wound went from oozing before the irrigation to bleeding in earnest.

She dabbed it with sterile gauze and covered the area with an anesthetic spray.

After giving the painkiller a minute to work, she held his arm, sutured his wound, giving him small, neat stitches, and then snipped the thread. She applied antibiotic ointment and put a self-adhesive gauze pad on to protect it.

"Finished," she said, tugging off the gloves and chucking them in the trash.

Thank goodness that was done.

Being so close to him, with all that bare skin exposed, and touching him had turned her insides molten. This was testing her sanity and tempting her in new ways.

She stepped around him to put away the supplies.

"Thank you." He caught her wrist and pulled her in between his legs.

As she leaned into his touch, her heart remembered the rule about keeping some physical distance with Aiden, but her libido seemed to have shredded the memo. She dragged her gaze down his sleek, tightly muscled torso to the unmistakable bulge tenting his towel.

How was that possible while getting stitches?

Then again, Aiden was the most remarkable man she knew.

Charlie looked up at him, her pulse beginning to race. Carnal images of them tangled up in bed together floated through her head.

Desire was etched on his handsome face, in the sexy grin on his full mouth. He exuded sex—raw, sheet-clenching sex—or standing this close to him, with his body on display and a bed a few stumbles behind her, simply made her think about all the ways they could pleasure each other.

For one night.

She pressed her palms to his smooth chest and wicked warmth spiraled through her. Touching him excited her; it was a heady intoxication, but she couldn't shake the wariness that came along with it. She was terrified to want this, terrified of how it'd change things.

He stroked her damp hair and caressed her face with the back of his hand. His eyes, glinting with sensual promise, blazed into hers, incinerating her doubts and fears one by one. She fought not to squirm while her thighs tingled and every cell in her body perked up.

She wanted to blame this craving to feel his skin

on hers, this inexplicable draw to him, on the shots of vodka, on their near-death experiences.

But that was a lie too big even for her to swallow.

He wrapped his arm around her waist and brought her flush against him. With the pad of his thumb he traced a searing path across her lips. The heat of contact had her melting faster than butter in a hot skillet.

His eyes were so dark and fathomless she could dive in and never find the bottom.

The air was thick and heavy, charged with an undeniable current like flammable gas. One lit match was all it would take for a total disaster.

Hell, static electricity might do it.

"I want you." His voice was husky and full of gravelly heat.

Sparks of arousal shivered along her nerves. As intense as their attraction was, there was understanding, too, a comfort in being known, and she had to protect that at all costs.

"I've had a lot to drink," she said. "If I don't remember this tomorrow, promise not to hold it against me."

Lies. Well, she did have a few shots, but she was far from toasted, and she'd remember every scintillating detail of being with this man. But they needed an out, a sort of parachute. Pull the rip cord and they'd land safely, nothing broken, and go back to normal.

His eyes narrowed, sending unease skittering down her spine. He studied her, and she met his measuring gaze, unblinkingly.

"So you'd only sleep with me if you could call it a slipup," he finally said, and she stilled at his tone, the gravity in his eyes. "Blame it on too much alcohol?"

"Yes. No. I don't know." Damn, he knew her too

well. But he made it sound horrible and unforgivable. A betrayal of the worst kind. "You're curious about what it'd be like for us to have sex. I am, too, but once our curiosity is satisfied, we need to be able to go back to the way things were."

"Why do things need to go back? Why can't they move forward? As nature intended. I'm not curious about sleeping with you. I'm *interested* in *being* with you."

Her heart tripped into her throat as she felt the blood drain from her face. For a moment she didn't know what to say, silence swelling between them, but she gathered what wits she had left. "How many people have successful relationships in our office? How many are divorced, separated? How many in SOG, where we're constantly on call and have to drop everything to respond in six hours? This job, this lifestyle isn't conducive to matrimony or monogamy."

He dropped his hand from her face.

"The odds of anything romantic between us succeeding are bad enough," she added, her mind spinning, redirecting wherever she could that didn't lead to the painful truth. "If we became a couple it would muck up work."

"How?"

"At Albatross's house, you ordered me to take cover in the refrigerator while you took point and ran into the fray."

"I ordered you to protect him."

"Would you have done that if I were a man?"

"Yes! Because that's who I am. I can't help it. I'm not sexist, Charlie."

"What about at the bar? How you wanted me to stay in the car. Are you going to try and deny that, too?"

He blinked at her. "I'd never ask you to stop doing a job you're good at, one you love. Relationships are scary. They're a gamble. But I like our odds. I'd bet everything I have on us."

"What we have is special and I don't want to lose it. You're my—"

"Yeah, best friend. I know," he scoffed, looking away from her.

"No, you don't know. You're more than my best friend." She pressed a palm to his cheek, turning his head until their eyes met. "You're my only friend. You're my person." A tiny voice in the back of her head warned that she was getting in too deep, but she kept going. "The one I confide in, hang out with. You're my emergency contact, for God's sakes."

His whole face twisted in utter disappointment.

She let him go. "Come hell or high water," she said, stalking back and forth in front of him, "I've got your back and I know you've got mine. You're my family, Aiden. You're my…" She swallowed the word *partner*. In every way except sexual he was, but fear overwhelmed her, and she pulled the rip cord. "You're my brother." The necessary lie stung her tongue, but it was for the good of them both. "Maybe you should think of me as a sister."

In an explosive move, Aiden swooped forward with such forceful urgency it drove her feet back. This was bad, bad, bad. He cupped her face in his hands, bringing her pacing to an abrupt stop. Without warning or hesitation, he pulled her mouth to his and kissed her.

The instant their lips touched, her thoughts scattered and the lies were lost in a hot vortex of total oblivion.

There was no stopping the shocked moan that slipped from her on a wave of arousal that floored her like an express train. His tongue swept across the seam of her lips and delved inside. His fingers slid into her hair as he drew her even closer, his mouth hot and possessive against hers, claiming a deeper taste.

She threw her arms around his neck, her nipples tightening, her body burning with scalding need for him.

He spun her around, backing her up against the wall, and rocked into her, their bodies straining, melding in perfect harmony.

The hard ridge of his erection pressed into her abdomen. A yearning ache thrummed between her thighs. He caressed her breast through the soft cotton, dragged his thumb across her nipple, but it wasn't enough. She wanted more.

As if reading her dirty mind, he dived into her robe and cupped her sex, palming her. Stoking her arousal.

Guilty pleasure blindsided her. Her body throbbed with painful, wet need.

She couldn't stop herself from rubbing against the delicious pressure of his hand and didn't want to.

This was foolish. Reckless. That registered in some obsolete part of her brain, but the electricity crackling between them overrode her thoughts.

There was only hunger centered on this man. She wanted him more than she wanted to breathe. All of him. Inside her, deep and fast and hard and rough.

Blood thudded against her eardrums and pulsed in her groin. "More, more." The words spilled from her mouth in a rough whisper.

She was condemned to hell. The upside was the road

was slippery and hopefully riddled with orgasms. If he kept this up, she'd have her first pretty soon.

His mouth left hers, gliding across her cheek, her jaw, to her carotid artery, where her pulse pounded wildly as she took ragged breaths, wanting to curl into him.

"I'm your brother, huh?" His voice, soft with menace, skated over her skin. "You sure as heck don't kiss me back like a sister."

Shock and hurt slapped her.

She very nearly picked up the gauntlet he threw down. But the one thing she was better at than fighting was running. And when your survival depended on it, you learned to run like the devil was chasing you.

"Out of all the excuses I imagined hearing from you, this one takes the cake," he said. Lust and anger etched his features into something dark and smoldering and dangerous. "Truly priceless. The worst part is, I think you're delusional enough to believe it." The harshness of his words stunned her heart, but she jerked out of his arms.

Her body mourned the loss of his male heat, his scorching touch.

"I'd give my right hand to get under your skin," he said, "to have you want me the way I want you. I've stood by for years, being there for you. Being *your person*. Loving you. Wanting you. I told myself that one day, when you were ready for a relationship, you would open your eyes to what was in front of you. Instead, you dated Nick. Not just a guy in the office, where I had to have it thrust in my face every damn day, but one of my friends. I had to hear about the details from both of you. Do you have any idea what that was like for me?"

After all he'd just said, the question was rhetorical, but he didn't let her off that easily.

"It gutted me, Charlie. And if by some chance the two of you had worked out, it would've broken my heart."

Guilt ripped her to pieces.

Aiden was twisting everything up inside of her into a giant choking knot.

"I wasn't serious about Nick." He was a friendly work associate that she passed her off-duty time with between the sheets. They'd hooked up until he started pushing to turn their superficial fun into a real relationship. She didn't do long-term with anyone. Living half a life wasn't so bad when the idea of anything else, anything more, seemed impossible, too far out of reach. "We didn't date. It was just sex. I never even stayed the night with him. He was a distraction." *From wanting you.* "I didn't sleep with him to hurt you."

"But you did hurt me!" The stricken look on his face was a knife in her chest. "Are you going to stand there and tell me that you didn't know how attracted I am to you? Are you going to deny that it's mutual?"

If she tried, a bolt of lightning would probably strike her. The intensity of their attraction was as strong as gravity. There were times when he'd give her a look that sent a current of raw desire racing under her skin, making her stomach dip and her breath grow shallow. Of course she knew.

Lowering her eyes, Charlie backed away.

"There's something I haven't told you." His voice grew quiet. "I was offered a position at Camp Beauregard, as an instructor. I was torn about taking it because I was holding on to hope. About us. I think after we clear our names and go back, I'm going to accept the position."

Panic slithered up her spine and coiled in her gut. "No. No, no." A fierce longing shook her to the core. "You can't be serious." He wanted to leave her. "Why?"

"Because I can't keep pretending that this is platonic when it's anything but. My mind files away all these details about you. The way you move, your smile, the smell of you, that defiant way you hike your chin, the sexy hollow of your throat, the curve at the small of your back, creating a sick map of you. One that I see and want to touch that leads me back to you when I'm with someone else." Naked emotion passed over his carved features and he withered in front of her.

She stared at him, sad desperation flooding her veins.

"As long as I continue to be your person," he said, "I'll never be able to move on from you. It'd be impossible to fall in love with anyone else. I want to get married, have a family, children."

A sinkhole opened inside her, rattling her to the very foundation of her soul. *Children.* Something she'd never be able to give him or anyone else.

"I need all those things. I wanted them with you." He shook his head. "But I can see now that's never going to happen."

It was too much and not enough. "Aiden…"

He waited, the hope in his eyes glaring.

Tension swelled in the room around them. Her mouth opened, but no sound came out. She didn't know what to say to keep from losing him. The weight of that inevitability settled in her chest.

"Get some sleep," he snapped. "We've got a long

day ahead of us." He stormed into the bathroom and shut the door.

Her heart hammered, her brain reeling.

The dread inside her shot to a higher pitch and her muscles turned to gelatin. Charlie sank down on the bed, trying to piece together what had started it all, how everything had spun out of her control. Her only answer—the kiss they'd shared earlier.

They'd opened Pandora's box back in the car when their lips had locked, and they'd tasted the passion burning between them.

A sudden realization struck her with such blunt force that it stole her breath. She was in love with Aiden. Not as a sister loved a brother, but as a woman loved a man.

And he was in love with her.

She'd been kidding herself all along that she could control this. What a fool she'd been.

Maybe she should tell him the truth. Why they couldn't be together. The real reason they'd never work.

A hurricane of conflicting emotions rioted inside her, making her eyes sting.

He'd stirred up a longing for something she couldn't have, to be someone that she couldn't—a mother…to be *his* in every sense of the word.

Her eyes watered, tears burning. She burned…ached for him. For the impossible.

Aiden threw open the bathroom door. He was dressed as he stomped out, not casting a single glance at her. "I need some air. I can't breathe."

Before she could utter a word, he was gone.

Chapter Twelve

His hands in fists at his sides, Aiden stormed out of the hotel as desire pounded through him. His straining erection was painful, and his head was a mess.

He was a complete wreck and Charlie was what he needed to fix it. She was like a drug, a habit he couldn't kick no matter the side effects or warnings or devastation.

Sleeping with her would've only made the addiction worse.

Aiden knew this and still he wanted her. Needed her. He was a lost man.

His lungs heaved with a foreign anger. Stalking down the street, he was furious. At himself. Not at her. It wasn't her fault any more than it was heroin's or meth's for a person needing that fix, again and again.

He never should've put her in that position back in the hotel room. Never should've thrown the job offer in her face that way.

It wasn't like him to be cruel. Even if she had been cruel first.

You're my brother. Maybe you should think of me as a sister.

A stab speared through his chest as he recalled her words. Her lies. It made him sick to his stomach.

He punched the air and swore under his breath, his mind, his body, every inch of him humming with the memory of kissing her, stroking her hot wetness between her thighs. How good she'd felt, how receptive she'd been, turned on by him so quickly. How much he'd wanted to slip inside her and bury himself in her heart.

Madness whirled around in his head, a firestorm of pent-up sexual frustration consuming him. He was disgusted with himself for how he'd spoken to her. Touched her. A part of him felt as if he'd violated their friendship. The other part felt like he hadn't gone far enough.

What was wrong with him?

Aiden scrubbed his hand over his face. The musky scent of Charlie filled his nostrils, inflamed his blood. Stoked the madness swelling in his skull.

He should've washed his stupid hands, but he'd been fired up and in such a rush to get out of the hotel room that it was a miracle he'd taken the time to get dressed.

Desperate to shake himself free of this misery, he needed to focus on the trouble they were in, on finding a solution out of it. On anything except the always present chemistry between them. Chemistry that'd sparked the day they met.

A fresh clutch of pain tightened in his chest.

Stopping, he found himself standing in front of another hotel. He went inside and used the bathroom off the lobby, soaping up his hands twice and scrubbing them clean.

He threw away the paper towels and rubbed the outline of the flash drive in his pocket. They had no clue exactly what was on it. Finding out might give him some idea what their next step should be.

This situation wasn't going to fix itself, and dwelling on Charlie wasn't helping.

He walked up to the concierge desk as if he was a guest staying there. "Hi. Where's the business center?"

The clerk directed him to a comfy lounge with living room furniture, computers and printers. The lounge flowed into a twenty-four-hour coffee shop. Since it was communal space, the Wi-Fi was free, and he wasn't even asked for a room number to access the internet.

After he bought coffee and a premade packaged sandwich from the coffee bar, he settled in at one of the computers for a long haul. It'd take time to carefully sift through the drive. If they had any hope of winning this, they needed to know who they were going up against.

He had to concentrate on their current problem. Clearing their names, which also meant finding Edgar, alive.

Then he'd take the job as an instructor. Go to Camp Beauregard. *Rehab.* The only way to get over Charlie... Killinger. That was how he'd think of her from now on.

And she'd have to find a new emergency contact.

SITTING IN THE passenger's seat of the Crown Vic, Devlin sipped his hot coffee, grateful for the shades shielding his eyes from the early-morning light.

"That should do it," Detective Carol Jenkins said, switching off the recorder on the dash. "Thanks for answering all of my follow-up questions."

"No problem. I just want to help in any way I can. It's awful what those marshals did."

"Yeah." Detective Jenkins nodded. "It makes everyone in law enforcement look bad."

"The one thing I can't stand is a dirty cop. Or marshal, for that matter." He took another hit of much-needed caffeine, trying not to choke on his lies. At 7:00 a.m., his brain was still fuzzy, but deception came naturally to him. No effort or thought required. "Thank you for the lift to the airport and for understanding about me needing to catch an earlier flight."

"Of course. Who hasn't had a family emergency? I'm sorry to hear about your brother-in-law's heart attack."

When Jeff had called Devlin, hysterical, his brother-in-law had sounded as if he was going to have an actual coronary. Those marshals had some audacity to waltz into their place filled with cops and beat Jeff for information. At least they only broke his finger. They could've broken his arm.

The good news was his plan was working.

His worst-case scenario was Yazzie and Killinger being arrested. The flash drive seized. Stuff went missing from evidence rooms more often than civilians would imagine. Hell, if he could sneak out weapons and bricks of cocaine, he would've found a way to smuggle out a tiny thumb drive.

But luck was on his side. The best-case scenario was in play. The marshals were virtually bringing the drive to him. He owned that city.

Now that he knew they were there, he'd find them.

Smoke them out if necessary while Devlin's friend here in San Diego would tie up the loose end of the wife at Mission Medical.

"Detective, if you've got any other questions, I'm happy to answer them over the phone or even Skype."

She nodded, pulling up to the terminal. "What time does your plane land?"

"I'll be home by lunchtime. I'll take my sister out for a bite to eat, give her a break from the hospital." He'd have lunch all right, but not with his sister. His first stop would be Avido's, to ensure Big Bill made the initial payment.

"I wish I had a brother as thoughtful as you."

He shrugged. "I do what I can."

"I hope your brother-in-law gets out of ICU and recovers."

"Thanks. We're all fighters in my family." The strong survived. "I've got a good feeling that he's going to pull through."

It was late morning by the time Aiden finished reviewing the evidence Edgar had hidden. After asking the concierge where he could buy a USB nearby, he dashed down a block and bought one. This city was great. Everything at his fingertips.

There was enough information on the drive to fill an encyclopedia. He copied about a chapter's worth to the new memory stick and printed some choice documents on Walsh and his hostile business partner, Romero, that, when put in the right hands, would send them to prison for a very long time.

On his way back to the hotel, Aiden swung by a restaurant. Grabbed breakfast sandwiches, beignets and coffee with chicory, black for *Killinger* and au lait for him.

He put his key card in the slot. The little green lights flashed, the lock released, and he opened their room door.

Charlie was dressed and on her feet, moving toward

him before the door shut behind him. "Where have you been? Are you all right? I've been worried sick about you. I checked the business center and the front desk to see if you got your own room."

Good thing he'd used a computer at a different hotel. Otherwise he would've got sidetracked. He set the documents on the bed and handed her a coffee and a bag with her sandwich and half the order of beignets.

"What is this?" she asked, sounding bewildered.

"Breakfast and leverage," he said coolly, nodding to the pages.

She stared at him wide-eyed. "Where did you sleep?"

"Didn't. You?"

She shook her head, her eyes looking haunted.

He bit into a beignet. Warm and deep-fried and sweet, it hit the spot. He held up the pastry. "You should try one. You'll like it, Killinger."

She flinched at his use of her last name and grew overtly edgy.

If she wanted to play the he-was-her-brother game, he'd do her one better and play the they-were-only-partners game.

"We're going to get Albatross back," he said, trying to prevent things from getting unbearably awkward.

They were forced to be together, but he'd get his own room or, to conserve their limited cash, at least switch to double beds. The more professional he kept their interaction, the easier it'd make things.

No compromising positions. No embarrassing confessions. No kissing. No touching.

Stick to business and the monumental task at hand.

"How?" she asked.

"Blackmail."

For the rest of the morning, they walked on eggshells around each other and avoided eye contact as he showed her the printouts and they hashed out a quasi plan.

They had to buy Edgar time and they had the power to do it. That was the easy part.

The rest would be tricky. There were too many variables beyond their control to know if it'd work. They had everything to lose, but it was their best chance. The key to success was proper redirection. Fortunately, Killinger was an expert at it and he was a quick learner.

He picked up the phone and dialed a number he'd written down last night.

The phone rang and was answered. "You've reached the FBI field office of New Orleans."

He listened to the automated menu and hit the number for the prompt that he wanted. As luck would have it, someone answered on a Saturday. "This is Agent Simmons. How can I help you?"

"Hello, I'm calling from the US Marshals office. I was wondering if Agent Bryan McCaffrey was in today," Aiden said, inquiring about the special agent in charge of the office, according to the website.

Most FBI field offices were open seven days a week and some of the larger ones worked around the clock. With a smaller office such as New Orleans, there was no telling if the boss would be in on a Saturday.

"Yes, sir. He is. May I ask what this call is regarding?"

"I had some questions following a hunch on a case I'm working and wanted to discuss something with him." Aiden didn't actually want to talk to McCaffrey; he'd called only to find out his schedule for the day. "On second thought, something just occurred to me.

I think I should get some additional information first, get my ducks in a row before I bother him. How late is he going to be there today?"

"Well, he works from seven to seven."

"Is he just committed or going through a divorce?" Aiden asked, recalling that when Draper had been hired to take over the San Diego office, he had been going through a divorce and had worked twelve- to sixteen-hour days, as well.

"Both," the agent said. "Can I get your name to pass along to him? I'll give him a heads-up to expect a call later."

"Thank you." Aiden hung up and nodded to Charlie. "He'll be in. Let's go."

They left the hotel and scouted the area for a significant tourist site that drew a lot of foot traffic and offered multiple lines of sight.

Jackson Square was perfect. Fifteen-minute walk from the hotel. A wide-open space that could be watched from across the street at the outdoor Café du Monde.

Aiden purchased a postcard featuring the square from a shop, along with four envelopes and a pen. On the back of the postcard he wrote:

If you want the rest of the evidence, have the Assistant Special Agent in Charge who is building a case on Bill Walsh here, wearing a red hat and red shirt, standing next to the cluster of palm trees on the southwest corner of the Andrew Jackson statue. Noon. Sunday.

Aiden circled the specific tree on the card, silently thanking Jeff Landau for the tip that Big Bill was under federal surveillance. He put the postcard and two sheets from the pages that he'd printed out in an envelope, giving a tidbit of incriminating evidence on Walsh and

Romero. Not enough for an arrest and conviction, just a taste to whet the appetite for more.

"They'll check for prints and get results in less than twenty-four hours," Charlie said.

"That's what I'm counting on. It'll save time when we make contact."

Charlie rubbed her hand across the envelope, getting her prints on it, as well. He addressed it to Bryan Mc-Caffrey and marked it Extremely Urgent.

Then he put the flash drive with all the information in a padded envelope and made it out to the attorney general at the Department of Justice in Washington, DC. They couldn't risk hanging on to the drive when it was worth millions and could put half a dozen criminals behind bars.

The rest of the paperwork he divided between the last two envelopes. One labeled for Romero. The other for Walsh. Those two they'd deliver in person. The others had to be mailed.

New Orleans was such a convenient city. A courier service that guaranteed same-day delivery was located off Canal Street and was only a ten-minute jaunt on foot.

They sent the envelope to Special Agent McCaffrey with signature required for delivery. He'd get it no later than 4:00 p.m. that day. Twenty hours was plenty of time for McCaffrey to arrange things with his subordinate who was covering Walsh.

Next was the package to the attorney general. They'd mail it from the post office, priority but not overnight, since they didn't want it to arrive until Tuesday no later than close of business, when their hand would've been played.

By then, they'd either have Edgar, be in police custody or be dead.

No matter their outcome, Walsh, Romero and every other scumbag on that flash drive was going to prison.

"What if McCaffrey doesn't go for it?" she asked, her cool, seemingly detached composure slipping. "What if an agent doesn't show tomorrow?"

"Chill out, Killinger." It would work. It had to. "Have a little faith."

What was the alternative? Expect the worst?

Not his style. He suspected that not only the agent covering Walsh would show but that the square would be swarming with federal agents tomorrow.

"We still don't know how to neutralize Devlin," she said. "He flies in tonight. He's going to find out that we're in town. If he doesn't already know."

Devlin was a wild card. A problem they didn't have a fix for yet. "Maybe we use the element of surprise. Get to him before he can cause any more trouble."

"How?" Aiden asked. "Nab him at the airport?"

They knew what flight he'd be on, seven o'clock from San Diego, and they knew what he looked like. Devlin wouldn't expect the preemptive strike. "Yeah, maybe."

One step at a time. First, they needed to deliver the other two envelopes. Throw out the bait and set the traps.

They walked to the casino in silence, resigned to their neutral corners, with the giant elephant wedged between them. She didn't seem to want to discuss it any more than he did.

Fine with him. *We just need to get through this and come out the other side.*

Carrying crowbars and baseball bats into the casino

was a no-go. Even if they had guns, getting them inside would've been tough.

The Windfall was large and active and bristling with energy. Slot machines clinked off to one side. On the other, patrons gathered around card and craps tables and a roulette wheel. Shouted. Whooped. Cheered. Groaned. It was an overwhelming scene straight out of Vegas.

"Suggestions, Killinger?" he asked.

She stiffened and looked around. Her gaze was directed at anything other than him. "I don't like the idea of an enclosed office surrounded by guards. There might be a better option. I'll ask."

They subtly slipped their earpieces in and Killinger fluffed her hair to cover hers. Aiden planned to keep his distance.

Killinger stopped a cocktail waitress who was carrying a tray of empty glasses. "Hey, I'm looking to catch Enzo Romero and Big Bill Walsh, discreetly," she said, the comms device allowing Aiden to hear everything. "To pass along some information. I'd prefer not to get trapped in a difficult position in an office behind a locked door, with some dude's hand shoved down my shirt, if you know what I mean."

The buxom waitress smiled. "Believe me, I get it. Enzo's right over there." She pointed to a man in a fancy suit in the poker room. "And Big Bill is at Avido's this time of day. But ask to see him at the bar, otherwise they'll send you to his office there."

"Thanks." Killinger handed her a hundred bucks. "How do I get to Avido's?"

The waitress gave directions and pocketed the easy cash.

"I count two bodyguards in Enzo's vicinity," Killinger said. "Give me his envelope. I'll get it to him without drawing too much attention. They won't see me as a threat."

He agreed and handed over the envelope. The contents would show Romero what type of damning information they had on him.

Killinger sauntered into the poker room and Aiden stayed across the walkway where he could keep an eye on her. She strode right up to Enzo Romero and proffered the sealed white envelope. "You're a very powerful man with a lot of influence and muscle, and I'm looking to make a deal. Help me get what I want and all the information I have is yours."

Enzo eyed her from head to toe, then opened the envelope and looked over the single page. His brows lifted. "What do you want?"

"Not money." She pulled on a smile smooth as cold butter. "I'll call you tomorrow with details."

Enzo reached into his suit jacket pocket, whipped out a card and handed it to her. "My private number. Can I buy you a drink?"

"Thank you." She took the card. "But it's a little early in the day for me." She turned and strutted out of the poker room.

Enzo signaled to one of his guards, who took off after Killinger.

In turn, Aiden was right behind him.

Killinger went to the ladies' room. The guard had the audacity to follow her inside. Aiden had no shame in joining the party.

He shoved through the door fast. As expected, the bodyguard turned and half stepped back, a fluid quarter circle.

Aiden threw a sharp left hook, catching him hard on the ear. The guy's head snapped sideways as Aiden was already launching a right uppercut that hit him under the chin.

The guard wobbled and swayed, staying on his feet. Killinger jumped up behind him and locked her elbow around his throat in a headlock.

Aiden could've been a referee in a ring, counting down the knockout.

Five seconds, and the bodyguard was out cold.

One baited hook had been dropped for Romero.

Time to cast an irresistible, shiny lure for Walsh.

Chapter Thirteen

Devlin shook Tommy's hand with a pat on the shoulder and strode to the small office in the back of Avido's.

Inside, Big Bill waved for him to come in. "Can I get you some lunch?" he asked, sprinkling salt on his chicken.

The food smelled wonderful and everything Devlin had ever eaten there had been tasty, but he wanted to get down to business. "I'm good." He took a seat in one of the leather chairs facing the desk.

Bill set the white porcelain shaker down and took a bite of his food. "What's the status?"

"Is this place clean?" Devlin asked, referring to listening devices. Bill's FBI problem was worse than an infestation of roaches.

"Yeah." Bill nodded. "Tommy swept it this morning."

"The boys are in Louisiana," Devlin said. "They checked in with me outside of Lake Charles. Your package can be delivered by five, if you'd like."

Bill leaned back in his chair, a satisfied grin tugging at his mouth. "I'd like that very much."

"Where?"

Without hesitation and with plenty of zeal, as if he'd given it a lot of thought, perhaps the only thing he'd thought of, Bill said, "Same place we bring the girls through."

The old port. Bill trafficked young women through on boats in shipping containers. The Coast Guard never went near it, the police were paid to steer clear, and the feds didn't have a clue Bill used it. A good spot for delivery and whatever else Bill had in store for the package.

"What about the information I need?" Bill cut another piece of chicken and chewed.

"There's a flash drive that supposedly has everything you could possibly want on it, but the package lost it. I'm working on getting it back."

"How in the hell are you going to do that?" Bill asked around the food in his mouth.

Devlin crossed his legs and folded his hands, letting his confidence shine through. He had this under control. "The flash drive is in New Orleans."

"I'm not tracking." Bill dropped his fork and wiped his mouth with a napkin. "Explain."

"Two marshals that were protecting the package have it. Aiden Yazzie and Charlotte Killinger. I framed them for the murder of one of their own and a local cop. Under the heat, they ran. I made sure to drop bread crumbs that led to me. They followed them and they're here. In New Orleans."

"How are you going to get the drive from them?"

"Leave that to me." One way or another, Devlin would get it and take care of them permanently. "I want the first payment. Three and a half million. Wired now to the same offshore account I used last time."

"Two million," Bill said flatly and took a long, hearty sip of his stout beer.

"Your math must be fuzzy. Seven million for the package alive. Half of seven is three and a half."

"Where's my proof of life?" Bill gestured dramatically around the office. "I have no doubt that you have him, but Edgar might've caught a stray bullet during the kidnapping and could be dead, for all I know. Two now. Five on delivery."

Devlin reached into his jacket pocket, past his holstered gun, took out a burner phone and dialed.

It rang twice. "What's up, D?" Tate asked. "We get paid?"

"We need proof of life. Send it now." Devlin disconnected. Eight seconds later, the phone buzzed. Devlin opened the text, bringing up a picture of the package.

His wrists and mouth were duct-taped, and he was wide-eyed with terror. A receipt from a gas station, with today's date and time stamp, was next to his head.

Devlin held up the phone, the picture facing out. He zoomed in on the receipt and then refocused on the package's horrified face.

Evil amusement lit up Bill's eyes as he flashed a Cheshire cat grin. "Three and a half million it is."

Their half-baked plan might get them both killed.

At least death would put her out of her misery, but the thought of anything bad happening to Aiden made Charlie physically ill. She could tolerate a lot, but not that.

She walked beside Aiden down quiet St. Philip Street in the heart of the French Quarter. The city was steeped in history, practically dripping with it. Nineteenth-century homes that lined the road resembled colorful dollhouses. The cheery, built-to-withstand-anything atmosphere was a stark contrast to their predicament and the current status of their friendship.

Charged silence stretched between them, prickling her nerves.

When she sidestepped a stray glass bottle as an excuse to move closer to Aiden, their hands brushed. He recoiled as if he couldn't bear the slightest physical contact with her and quickened his pace.

A cold shroud settled around her despite the sweltering temperature. With her stomach churning, she caught up and matched his stride.

She was a real mess, emotions running wild, and she couldn't let any of it show.

It was one bad thing after another. Losing a witness, being framed for the murder of a colleague, no loyalty from a shameful boss, and now being on the run. Yet the distance from Aiden clung to her like a choking vine, tightening her throat, squeezing her chest and making it hard to breathe.

Finally, they reached Bourbon and turned left. The famous bustling street vibrated with crackling energy. The cacophony of laughter, conversations, jazz and rap music was an overwhelming relief.

They strode through the throng of people, looking for Avido's Restaurant, where they hoped to find Big Bill Walsh and survive the encounter.

Charlie hated fumbling her way through something on a wing and a prayer and unarmed.

At any rate, she wasn't stuck in this alone. She had Aiden. There wasn't a better person to have at her side if she was in trouble.

Even if he was still so angry at her that he hadn't looked at her since they'd left the hotel.

Not only had she deeply hurt him, but she'd also disappointed him.

If she could take back ever sleeping with Nick last year, she would. It had meant nothing to her, whereas Aiden meant everything. Not that it would change anything now.

A chasm had opened between them last night when he'd poured out his heart to her and she hadn't been fully forthcoming in return. All this time, she'd had him locked tight in the friend zone, never daring to jeopardize their precious bond by sleeping with him, and it had only pushed him away to the point he wanted to leave her. Take the job here in Louisiana, of all places, at Camp Beauregard.

It was like some twisted self-fulfilling prophecy.

There were some things that couldn't be fixed. Charlie feared that she and Aiden were one of them. If she lost him, it would do more than break her heart. It would devastate her. The thought came with a knife-sharp pang, but she didn't break her stride.

She saw the sign for Avido's two doors down on the other side of the street. "There it is."

"I'd have to be blind to miss it," he said.

They couldn't walk into Big Bill's place like this—distracted and snapping at each other, their friendship fractured.

They needed to be the dynamic duo again if they were going to prevail with the deck stacked against them.

"Hey," she said, cupping his bare arm, stopping him from crossing the street. "We need to go in there as a united front."

He jerked away from her grasp. "We both want to

clear our names and walk out alive. That's about as united as we're going to get. Look, I'm sorry I crossed the line and kissed you. Touched you like that. It was a mistake."

Her heart sank and her jaw dropped.

"Let's forget it ever happened," he continued, "and move on. Stay focused on the mission. Okay, Killinger?"

Inwardly she cringed so hard it hurt every time he called her by her last name. "Stop it. Stop calling me that." It was driving her insane.

"Why? It's your name."

"Aiden, I—"

The door to Avido's opened, drawing both their gazes.

Charlie's heart nearly stopped. Frank Devlin walked out along with another man, tall, thickset, with a shaved head. Both had the telltale bulges of holstered weapons under their arm.

The timing couldn't have been worse.

"He's supposed to be on a plane later tonight. Not here. Now," she said.

Aiden took her by the elbow and turned away, shoving through a group of singing drunk guys.

"Watch it, buddy," one of them said.

A surge of adrenaline made her body buzz. Charlie craned around for a quick glance back.

Devlin spotted them. He tapped the burly guy beside him, pointed at them and then launched across the street.

Charlie took off without saying a word to Aiden. There was no need. She knew he followed right on her heels.

No matter how disconnected they were personally, they had always been in sync professionally.

They ran, forcing their way through the dense weekend crowd.

Aiden snatched her hand and cut down the side street, Orleans, dragging her with him. Then they ran at a flat-out sprint. Keeping up with him wasn't an issue. She could run like hell. The muggy air seemed to thicken. Breath sawed in and out of her lungs. Her heartbeat and the thump of their boots pounding on the pavement filled her ears.

Devlin and his surprisingly fast cohort came charging after them.

They had to shake those two men.

Straight ahead was a fenced-in garden behind a three-steepled church with a statue of Jesus in the center of the lawn, His arms upraised. This was the time to say a prayer if she knew any. The garden would do them little good, since it was a wide-open space and provided no cover.

Neither Charlie nor Aiden knew the city, while Devlin had home-field advantage and the entire police force on his side.

Charlie and Aiden reached the corner, their breaths coming hard. Looked left. Looked right. Split-second decision made.

They bolted down Pirates Alley and threaded in between strolling pedestrians. To one side of the thoroughfare was a towering church. To the other, the Cabildo and a Technicolor melee of lime green shutters, garish blue doors and neon yellow walls in the bowels of the city—all screaming that they had no clue where to run.

At the gaping mouth of the alley was a milling crowd. With a little luck, they might blend in, disappear.

On instinct, they turned to the left in unison, without hesitation, toward the church. Charlie made a beeline for the doors, hand in hand with Aiden.

It was locked. On the sign, the St. Louis Cathedral didn't open until five on Saturday.

Aiden tugged her up against him into a pocket of shadows in an alcove. Her heart jackhammered in her chest. Her brain engaged. Professional awareness was in high gear. Her determination like a cold iron bar. But there was no ignoring the feel of him against her, every spot where they touched, each lick of friction as they pressed closer. He was so solid and heavy, warmth radiating from his muscles flexing under her palms.

She wanted to shut off that part of her brain that picked up those details but also commit the particulars to memory. How steady and calm he was. The world could be falling apart, and he'd still be rock-solid.

The taller, stocky guy pounded past the front of the cathedral as vacationers taking photos in the pedestrian-only plaza out front inadvertently helped shield them. It probably didn't occur to him to look at the entrance since he knew the church would be closed.

For once, not knowing the area worked in their favor.

The thin peal of bells rang out, calling to saints and sinners alike. A circus atmosphere pulsed around them—meandering tourists, mimes, artists, street musicians, magicians, living statues painted in silver and gold, palmists and tarot readers selling glimpses of the future.

She looked up at Aiden. Their eyes locked.

He pressed a palm to her cheek and something she couldn't define shone in his eyes. "Come on."

Staying there wasn't an option. With two men canvassing the area—one a cop—they'd eventually be spotted.

They made a break for it, dashing through Jackson Square, around the equestrian statue and past a row of iron benches with dividers. They narrowly avoided a collision with a group of teenage girls who were running up to a row of fortune-tellers.

Aiden looked back. The squeeze of his hand tightening on hers told Charlie what she needed to know. One of the men wasn't far behind. Or probably, both were close.

There was no outrunning them. No place to hide where they wouldn't be found.

They had to make a stand.

Surprise would help, but hesitation would be fatal.

On Decatur, they blew by the French Market and ducked into a restaurant.

"Hello," said the hostess. "How many—"

Aiden pointed toward the back. "We're meeting people."

They strode through the restaurant.

At the sound of the hostess's voice again, Charlie looked to the front. Devlin breezed inside while the other guy went around the building.

Aiden pushed into the kitchen. "We do it here," he said, echoing her thoughts.

"As good a place as any." It was great to be on the same page. "Get out now, or you'll be shot," Charlie said to the gawking cooking crew. She waved them toward the back door with all the fierceness the Marine Corps had instilled in her.

The cooks scattered and fled.

Aiden switched off the lights, grabbed a steel meat tenderizer from the counter and stood against the wall beside one of the swing doors to the dining room.

The only light in the room came from the small window in the door and the five burners going on the stove.

Charlie's gaze flew around for something she could use as a weapon. Before she found one, Devlin rushed into the kitchen. His gun with a silencer attached was already drawn and at the ready.

Menace radiated from him as he leveled the 9 mm at her. Aiden sprang from his position, smashing the steel mallet on Devlin's wrist and knocking the weapon from his grasp.

Charlie grabbed a metal bowl of flour and spun on her heel when the back door flew open and the stocky guy stormed in. She tossed the flour into his face, followed by the bowl. Metal struck flesh with a resounding clang.

In her periphery, Aiden was going blow for blow with Devlin. A flurry of punches and kicks issued back and forth.

Charlie seized a large rolling pin from a workstation and swung it like a bat. The wood smacked into the man's solar plexus.

A loud grunt whooshed from the guy's mouth as he doubled over.

She threw another whack to his head. And another. She planned to keep thrashing him until he was either knocked out cold or the rolling pin broke, whichever came first.

The man dropped to the floor like a wet noodle.

Devlin bulldozed into Aiden, lifting him from the floor and hurling him into a shelving unit. Produce went flying, tumbling to the floor.

Landing a wicked left hook, Aiden forced Devlin off him. The two tussled. Aiden got Devlin facedown over the counter, wrenching one of his arms behind his back.

Charlie rushed to help subdue him.

Aiden's gaze snapped up at her. "No! Stay back," he said, bringing her to a halt.

It was in that second, maybe two, when Aiden's focus slipped slightly, that Devlin reared his head up and back, smashing his skull into Aiden's face. Her partner stumbled, his arms flailing. Devlin spun, throwing an elbow propelled by the momentum of his full weight to Aiden's head, and was on him like a violent storm.

Charlie surged forward, hoisting the rolling pin high.

Pivoting with his arm extended horizontally, Devlin hit her hard across the cheek. The force of his elbow moving fast ahead of two hundred pounds of mean muscle sent her head twisting around, her body spiraling and knocked to the floor.

Her skull slammed against the cold tile. Her breath left her lungs.

"Charlie!" Aiden cried.

The scuffle between Devlin and Aiden was all she could hear.

Fear mingled with blood. It was bitter and coppery in her mouth. She fought through the haze, needing to move, needing to help Aiden.

Her blurry vision cleared, and Charlie rolled onto her hands and knees. She scrambled to find a gun, scouring the floor, searching under the prep table.

Where did it go?

She made it to her feet, gasped in horror. Devlin had an arm locked around Aiden's throat, but her partner kicked off the wall, propelling them both into the work-table at the center of the room, sending them crashing to the floor.

Aiden and Devlin were duking it out on the floor, rolling around in a death match. The blows were furi-ous and fast. Aiden flipped him overhead, sending him hurtling against the stove.

As both men stood, Devlin's back was to Charlie. He reached behind into his jacket, going for the reserve weapon tucked in his waistband.

She snatched the pot of simmering water or broth from the fire and flung the piping hot liquid at him. Devlin howled and spun on her.

But Aiden threw a front kick that sent Devlin pitch-ing to the side over the flames. The sleeve of his light-weight jacket caught fire. With a quick presence of mind, Devlin snatched a pitcher of water and doused the flames with a faint sizzle.

Charlie knocked the gun loose from his hand with the hot pan while he was distracted.

The Beretta clattered to the floor. Aiden grabbed it and leveled the barrel at Devlin, who stood gape-mouthed, manic anger burning in his eyes.

Following Aiden's hand signal to move toward the door, Charlie backed up and stepped over the uncon-scious guy sprawled on the floor spread-eagle. She slowed and picked up his suppressed .45 from the cor-ner on the floor.

Devlin glared at them, his upper lip curling over his

teeth, his eyes wild and furious. "This isn't over," he growled.

"It better be." Aiden came up beside her and they backed through the door one at a time, her first. "Because if it's not, I'll kill you. That's not a threat. That's a promise." He slammed the door shut.

They hustled down the alley behind the restaurant. Aiden scooped up a dirty paper bag from the ground, dumped the contents and stowed the two guns inside.

There was one thing Charlie had to know. "Why didn't you kill that bast—"

"It's not who we are and it's the last thing we need. To kill a cop, even if he's a dirty one. Every officer will turn this city upside down and inside out looking for us."

Aiden was right. There were multiple witnesses able to clearly identify them. They didn't need the extra heat. Things were sweltering as it was.

"Let's hope we don't regret leaving him alive."

DEVLIN WAS SEETHING. His body began to shake with the rage building inside him, overshadowing the pain from his burns. He whipped out his personal phone.

But not to dial 911.

He'd officially report the incident, portraying them as stalkers trying to silence him, and have an all-points bulletin put out on the marshals, but it'd take his brothers-in-blue twenty minutes to get there and start looking for Yazzie and Killinger.

A faster response was required.

He pulled up the French Quarter Task Force app. An enterprise initiated and funded by a billionaire who wanted to make the city safer, using a crowdsourcing approach to crime. The FQTF was a private police patrol that could be summoned via a mobile app. Its monumental success encouraged the Louisiana State Police and surrounding parishes to use it, too.

The screen displayed a digitized map of the Quarter. A grid of seventy-eight city blocks. Green arrows indicated a member of the armed squad—off-duty cops rolling around in matte black smart cars at all hours, with the ability to respond to a crime in progress in under two minutes.

He plugged in the address of the restaurant he was standing in. Prepared for this type of scenario, he next uploaded the photos of Yazzie and Killinger the SDPD had been kind enough to share with him and typed the notification:

Armed and dangerous fugitives wanted for the murder of two law enforcement officers just tried to kill a local cop. They're on foot. Apprehend with caution. $25,000 REWARD.

He hit Enter.

A red dot appeared on his location. Pictures of the marshals flashed on the screen.

Ten green arrows in the vicinity immediately reacted and began zigzagging through the streets forming a perimeter, searching for them. And every citizen who had the app loaded on their phone would receive the alert and could submit updates on the whereabouts of the fugitives if they spotted them.

The entire city would be on the lookout for Yazzie and Killinger.

Chapter Fourteen

All the pieces on the board shifted with Devlin's early arrival. They had to adjust accordingly.

"We need to check out of the hotel," Aiden said. Get back their money for the second night, grab the meager clothing they had, his shirt, her jacket and their *weapons*. "Find someplace new, off the beaten path."

There was no doubt in Aiden's mind that Devlin would put out an all-points bulletin on them and was probably calling it in at that very moment.

Ahead at the corner they approached, two women in their late thirties were chatting and laughing as they looked at something on one of their mobile devices. The phone buzzed and emitted the jarring, high-pitched tone of a public safety alert. Another phone in the vicinity, somewhere behind them, did the same.

The women stopped talking and stared at the phone.

One of them, a redhead, swiped up on her screen.

The other, a black woman with long braids, gasped. "Twenty-five grand."

Both women frantically looked around, spinning in circles.

The redhead hit her friend and pointed at Aiden and Charlie. "That's them."

Aiden's chest clutched. He and Charlie froze for an instant and exchanged a glance. His mind raced to process what was happening, but there was no time to figure it out.

"That's them," the black woman said. "Report it."

The redhead started typing on her phone.

Charlie gestured to a massive open-air shopping complex that spanned several city blocks. They bolted across the street, skirting around vehicles.

A black smart car raced around the corner, lights flashing on top. Across the hood and side were the emblems of wings, a star and the words *FQ Task Force New Orleans Police Dept.*

Aiden and Charlie darted underneath the archway of the French Market as a second black task force car came zooming toward them from the other end of the street.

Rows of kiosks with vendors selling goods stretched out before them. They cut through the throng of shoppers, weaving their way around stands, hoping to blend in. Customers were absorbed in browsing and buying. Merchants focused on making sales.

The tawdry flea market was a veritable tourist trap, sitting at the edge of the Mississippi River, jam-packed with out-of-towners who didn't bat a lash at them.

Charlie spotted something, took his hand and led him to a bank of specialty shops. He didn't pull away. This was only about survival. Nothing more.

With his head on a swivel, looking for cops or anyone staring at them, he didn't understand what she was thinking until she pushed through the door of the store.

It was a costume shop.

"I'll wait out here." Not only to keep watch, but the store owner would be less likely to recognize or remember Charlie on her own if the proprietor had got the same notification.

Whatever alert the women across the street had received was about the two of them, together. So far, it didn't seem as if anyone in the market had noticed them. But that might not last much longer.

He glimpsed two cops working their way through the open-air enclave. More flashing lights stopped along the main street adjacent to the colonnade.

The seconds ticked down and his pulse kicked up.

Efficient as always, Charlie came out of the shop a minute later, carrying a bag. They pressed through the shopping colonnade, ducking into the first bathroom they came across—a unisex, single-occupancy room. She slipped on a short brown wig, tucking stray blond strands up inside, and a long-sleeve red shirt that transformed her into a stranger.

"Good work, Killinger," he said, her surname sliding from his lips before he could stop it.

This wasn't the time for him to deliberately rile her up by giving her the cold shoulder. To get through this, they had to act like a team, even if they weren't going to be partners for much longer.

To his surprise, she didn't roll her eyes or flinch or say anything at all. She dug into the bag and pulled out another hairpiece for him.

Charlie pulled the long black wig on Aiden. Her fingers caressed his forehead and cheeks as she straightened it, pulling errant strands from his face.

She took in a sharp breath, holding his gaze. Her piercing blue eyes were vibrant and inscrutable. It made his heart ache to look at her.

Then the ache deepened and spread when she cupped

his jaw, rose on the balls of her feet and pressed her lips to his.

The kiss was soft, closed-mouth, but searing.

Relief flooded him and he hated her for it, because there was no escaping that, deep down, he never wanted to be separated from her.

She settled back on her feet and glared at him. "Don't ever call me Killinger again." Then she threw a playful sucker punch to his gut.

Not hard enough to hurt, but a grunt escaped him nonetheless.

He glanced in the mirror. The straight shoulder-length hair reminded him of how he used to wear his own when he was much younger.

She handed him sunglasses, a green button-up that he threw over his T-shirt and a new ball cap since he'd lost his other one during the fight with Devlin.

They left the bathroom and headed for the closest exit.

The market was crawling with cops in every direction. If not for Charlie's quick thinking, there wouldn't have been any way for them to get out of the market without using violence.

Charlie linked her arm with his and they strolled by a police officer, making their way through the thick weekend crowd, beyond the souvenir stalls.

"Going back to the hotel is too risky," Charlie said. "We can't count on Dealing Dan not to report the car."

"Agreed."

Out on Decatur Street, a cab stopped right in front of a FQ Task Force police car and let out his passengers. The taxi light on the roof stayed illuminated. Charlie and Aiden got inside.

"Where to?" the driver asked.

"A motel," Charlie said. "Outside the French Quarter."

"Is a B and B okay?"

At B and Bs the owners chatted up their patrons, asked questions and shared stories. "No." Aiden shook his head. "A motel. We want privacy. Cheap. Clean. We don't need bells and whistles, but we do want outdoor access to the room."

The light-skinned black man eyed them in the rearview mirror. "I know you said no B and B, but if you're open to it, my aunt rents out a guest room above her garage to supplement her retirement. Outdoor access. Basic cable and Wi-Fi. I can promise it's clean. And my aunt is good people. She won't get in your business."

Aiden looked at Charlie and she nodded. "How much?" he asked.

"Eighty bucks a night. Breakfast and dinner are included in the price if you want it. She makes a mean crawfish étouffée. Better than anything you'll get in most restaurants."

If Dealing Dan had reported the car they'd rented, then the cops would have the names of their fake IDs. An off-the-books rented room was just what they needed. "Sounds perfect," Aiden said.

"How many nights?"

Charlie shrugged. "One or two."

The driver made a call on his cell. "Aunt Henri, it's me. I've got a couple of boarders for a night or two. Nice couple, looking for privacy, so don't go talking their ear off. Okay?" He listened for a minute, then said, "See you in a little bit."

Staying at a garage apartment meant they'd no longer have access to a computer in a hotel's business center, and they needed toiletries, as well. "Before we go to your aunt's place, do you mind swinging by a couple of stores? We could use some supplies."

"Sure. There's a shopping center on the way."

The cabbie let them out in front of a supersize discount retailer that had chains everywhere. Two doors down was a huge sporting goods store that from the outside appeared to be a hunter's dream.

Aiden handed the driver enough to cover the fare. "Keep the meter running. We'll be less than fifteen minutes." They got out of the car, and he turned to Charlie, but scanned their surroundings. "Faster if we separate." Not to mention easier, too, after that kiss she'd given him. He could use a little distance to clear his head. "I'll grab a computer, burner phones and toiletries. From there," he said, gesturing to sporting goods, "we need ammo, holsters and anything else you think will be useful. How are you on cash?"

"Running low, but I should have enough."

After using close to a thousand, he had plenty left from the three he'd withdrawn. She'd spend more on gear than he would in the supercenter. He peeled off five $100 bills for her.

Once they cleared their names, the Department of Justice should reimburse them for work expenses. Being on the run added up quick. If they'd been penniless, they would have been in the lurch.

Charlie pocketed the cash, looking like she wanted to say something, but he was grateful when she turned without a word and left. Eventually, they'd have to talk, but he was content to put off the conversation for as long as possible.

Inside the sprawling megastore, Aiden first grabbed toiletries they might need, since it was closest, and then headed for electronics. On the way, he threw a roll of flat black duct tape into the cart.

He found an assortment of cheap laptops and chose one with 4GB RAM for under a hundred bucks. It wouldn't be the fastest or offer much in terms of storage, but that was fine. Stopping at a display of cell phones on clearance, he picked two. Both flip-style, no-frills, bare-bones devices that didn't have GPS, which would make them harder to track. Then he added a couple of phone chargers to his pile.

At the twelve-minute mark, Aiden climbed back into the car. No one had been in line at the register in electronics and checking out there had expedited things. Less than sixty seconds later, Charlie left the sporting goods store carrying a tactical black backpack that was stuffed with goodies.

"You two aren't going to be any trouble, are you?" the driver asked as he watched Charlie walk to the car.

Her long, confident, I-am-in-command stride was distinctive, hinted at someone in law enforcement or the military, or a cocky criminal. The tactical backpack hiked high on her shoulder didn't help the image.

"I assure you the last thing we want is trouble." Aiden removed his sunglasses so the cabbie could see his eyes and hopefully his sincerity. "Just privacy and a little peace and quiet for a couple of nights."

The man considered it, and by the time Charlie hopped in, he nodded.

It didn't take long before the cabbie stopped in the driveway of a modest house that was outside the French Quarter but within reasonable walking distance.

An older lady with a poof of short white curls who resembled the driver was waiting for them. She wore pearls, a pencil skirt and a kind smile.

Aiden paid the remaining taxi fare and for waiting while they shopped, and they all climbed out.

"This here is my aunt Henriette Bordelon," the driver said. "Everyone calls her Henri."

Aiden shook her extended hand. "I'm Rudy and this is Priscilla," he said as Charlie shook her hand, as well. "It's kind of you to let us stay here, ma'am."

"My pleasure." She smiled, but glanced down at their hands, noticing they didn't have any luggage, only shopping bags and the backpack. "I hope it's okay if I collect payment in advance."

"No problem." Aiden gave her two hundred dollars.

"This is too much." She tried to hand back several bills.

"Please, keep it," Aiden said. "We heard you're an incredible cook. Consider it a tip in advance."

"Very generous of you." She beamed. "Dinner will be ready by six, but I can keep it warm for you as late as eleven. That's when my last show goes off and I turn in. Breakfast can be served anytime, except tomorrow. I go to church on Sundays. So it'll have to be before eight. If you have any allergies just let me know."

"Wonderful," Charlie said, "and no allergies for either of us. We'll eat anything."

The cabbie took the key from his aunt. "I'll walk them up and show them the place. Save you the trip."

Aiden and Charlie followed him up the steep exterior staircase. The structure was a good ten yards behind the main house, which had blooming flowers in all the beds and a well-maintained lawn. The garage apartment was far enough back to give them ample privacy.

The driver unlocked the door and handed Aiden the key.

A decent-sized studio, the place was as advertised. Simple. Clean. A rudimentary kitchen outfitted with the basics, including a coffee maker and take-out menus from places that delivered. Towels in the bathroom along with bodywash and shampoo.

It was more than they could've asked for.

But there was only one queen-size bed.

"Henri's number and the password for the Wi-Fi are next to the phone. I'm Junior, by the way. If you need a ride anywhere, day or night, give me a holler. Here's my card." Smiling, he offered one that Charlie took. "I'll get out of your hair now."

Nodding his thanks, Aiden set the shopping bags down on the counter.

Junior hurried out the door like he was trying hard not to take up too much time or be too friendly.

Aiden appreciated it.

Once Junior had cleared the stairs and the car door slammed closed, Charlie said, "We never got the envelope to Walsh and I don't think it's a good idea to go back to the restaurant."

She emptied the backpack on the counter, setting out a Smith and Wesson M&P 9 mm, shoulder holsters, tactical knives, zip ties, extra clips, and ammo for the guns, which they had three of, including the ones they took from Devlin and his buddy.

In Louisiana, no state permit, driver's license, firearm registration or background check was required, and by the looks of the supplies, no magazine capacity restriction, either. He wasn't complaining. This was the perfect state if you were a gun enthusiast or an outlaw.

An expandable baton made of strong, durable seamless alloy steel rolled along the counter as she pulled out a few more items that looked more suited for camping than their needs.

Taking off the sunglasses and wig, Aiden sat on the bed and scratched his head. "If it wasn't Walsh who texted the hit men in San Diego, then it was one of his guys. Either way, he'd get a message if we sent one."

"Then let's do it."

Aiden tore open the sealed envelope and laid the documents on the bed. He snapped a picture of each and sent them to the New Orleans number in the phone along with a text.

We have the flash drive with hard evidence on you and your friends.

Want to trade? Or do you want to go to prison?

"That'll get Walsh's attention," Aiden said. No need to rush the *ask*. Walsh was willing to pay millions to torture Edgar. They had time to play their hand the proper way, but not much. "Now we wait." He glanced at the clock. "We've got a couple of hours until dinner. I'm going to get some shut-eye."

Charlie removed her wig and the tomato-red shirt. "Can we talk?"

"Nothing else to say. We covered it last night." He tugged off his boots and sighed in relief. "I've been pushing for over thirty hours and it's been a tough day. I just want to take a nap. We can talk over dinner if necessary. Okay?"

Charlie hung her head. "Sure." She went to the bathroom and closed the door.

The shower started.

Aiden lay down, facing a wall and nightstand, fully dressed, and stared at the clock. He knew he needed to sleep, but he was restless and edgy. Too amped up to close his eyes or to relax.

His thoughts were a whirlwind and his emotions were all over the place before Charlie had kissed him in the market, and at the moment, they threatened to call the shots, but he refused to let them mess with his head.

Flopping onto his back, he stared at the ceiling. The curtains were too thin. The room was too bright. The sun was too hot. The room was too stuffy.

He looked back at the clock on the nightstand. Charlie had been in there a long time. She'd taken five minutes last night and now had been in the bathroom for close to thirty.

It wasn't his business. She wasn't his business. If she wanted to spend three hours in the bathroom, that was her prerogative. *Have at it. Use all the hot water. I don't care.*

Going on close to an hour, he admitted he was getting worried. Tempted even to knock on the door and ask if she needed anything. But nope.

He. Would. Not.

Finally, the water stopped; movement in the bathroom. He rolled onto his side, ensuring his back would be to her when she came out.

The door opened. Aiden shut his eyes, stilled his body, pretending to be asleep.

Charlie padded around the foot of the bed. Based on the sound, she was barefoot.

The mattress sank as she sat and lay down. His pulse skyrocketed, but he forced himself to take slow, even breaths. Forced himself not to move beyond the rise and fall of his chest.

"Aiden? Are you awake?"

It crossed his mind not to respond, to keep feigning sleep, but pretending for years that he wasn't in love with her and that whomever she slept with didn't bother him had only made things worse—throwing gasoline on the fire that had torched their friendship.

"I'm up," he said, letting every drop of irritation that he felt leak into his tone.

The mattress shook as she scooted closer and clasped his arm. "Aiden. Please. Look at me."

But he couldn't. Listening was one thing, but he didn't have the strength to look at her and keep a rein on his emotions.

"I lied—" Charlie's voice was soft, quiet "—when I said I think of you as a brother."

Tell him something he didn't know.

"I'm sorry I slept with Nick," she said. "It wasn't fair to you."

No, it wasn't, but he was guilty of a far greater wrong by not telling her that he loved her and not telling Nick to back off.

"If I could undo it, I would," she said. "You don't have to worry about getting under my skin. You already are."

A flutter of hope beat inside him. Was she saying what he longed to hear?

Confessions were dangerous; they exposed a person, made them vulnerable.

Charlie would give him some *but*, some out, an excuse in the end to protect herself. He just had to wait for it.

"Please, look at me," she said, her tone soft. He didn't move, and she squeezed his arm. "Aiden...for me, home isn't a place or a house. It's you. You're home for me. I love you and I don't want to lose you."

His heart kicked hard in his chest. His first instinct was to look at her, make her say it again while meeting his eyes. But the expectation of disappointment inextricably tied to this miraculous admission from her made him sick. With sadness. With anger. With love.

Lovesick.

Wait for it.

Her voice grew brittle and her hand fell from his arm. "But..."

A lead weight dropped in the pit of his stomach. Everything inside him tensed. *Here it comes.*

"I can't give you happily-ever-after. A family. All the things your parents had. I can't have children." Her words stalled time, stilled the beating of his heart.

For a nanosecond.

He rolled over and faced her.

She was wrapped in a towel, stripped of all her defenses. Her gaze lifted to his, her eyes pink and her face flushed like she'd been crying in the shower. He read the misery and fear in her unguarded expression, saw the icy bravado melt, and he took her hand in his.

"I had endometriosis. Nothing worked to help, and I had to have a full hysterectomy. I know I'm damaged, and I don't mean just the surgery. You can have everything you want. A great wife. Kids. The kind of family your parents had. Big and loving and warm. But not with me," she said, her voice cracking. Tears leaked from her eyes, a pinch of pain between her brows, the strain of sorrow pursing her lips together.

He wiped at her tears with his thumb, slid his palm over her hair, his heart aching for her. For them both.

"I want you to have that," she said. "You deserve it. More than anyone that I know. Any woman would be lucky to have you and you'll make a fantastic dad one day. The absolute best."

Neither of them breathed for what seemed like an eternity.

"Why didn't you tell me?" he asked in a whisper.

"I tried. Once, when you took me home for your mom's funeral."

He remembered the moment she was talking about. They'd been sitting on the porch, watching his nieces and nephews play in the yard. He'd gone on and on about how much he wanted a big family—four or five kids. To be a good dad like his own father.

His sister had given Charlie her youngest to hold. Charlie held the baby close to her chest, rocking him. He'd imagined marrying her, how beautiful she'd be pregnant, her belly heavy and round, her face glowing, her holding a baby that was a little bit of him and a little bit of her one day on that very porch. He'd envisioned their life together, happy and playful and satisfied, side by side, growing gray and old together.

She'd turned so somber that he'd put his arm around her and waited. For her to share. That was what he did. Gave her space, showed her patience until it hurt. She'd put her head on his shoulder and he'd sensed she'd been close.

"That afternoon on the porch," he said. "But my

brother asked me to go horseback riding. You insisted that I should, and I went with him."

Charlie nodded. More hot tears streamed down her cheeks.

He'd taken it as a sign of progress when she'd chosen to go home with him, that they were headed to the next level, but he realized he'd been wrong once he got back from riding with his brother. She'd left. Packed and taken a taxi to the airport. Given his family some excuse and had asked them to pass along the message that she'd see him back in San Diego.

He'd been shocked. Confused. Unbelievably hurt. Half tempted to run after her and demand an explanation like a lovesick fool, which he didn't want to be, and had chalked it up to Charlie being Charlie.

It all made sense now.

Aiden kissed her cheeks and wrapped his arm around her, bringing her in close. Held her tight, soothing her until she stopped crying. "I should've gone after you. To the airport. Made you talk to me and hashed it out then and there. It would've saved us so much time." So much grief.

"I'm sorry. You could've moved on sooner."

He pulled her deeper into his arms, cradled her head against his chest. "There is no moving on from you."

"Didn't you hear what I said?" She trembled against him and he held her tighter. "I can't give you a family. You want kids so badly."

"I want you more. You're my family. I love you, Charlie. The only future I want is one with you."

She shifted away, lifting her head. A tear slid down her cheek as she stared at him, lips parted. "No. You're supposed to understand. You're supposed to let me go."

"I'll never let you go. I'll always choose you."

"Aiden, I won't deny you—"

He stole her words with his mouth and kissed her.

Chapter Fifteen

His lips brushed over hers in a gentle, sweeping caress that made Charlie's heart turn over in her chest as he swallowed her objections. The kiss was raw and open and full of honesty.

She wanted Aiden to have the whole world. His greatest desires.

Not to choose her over having the family he wanted.

Aiden dragged his mouth across her cheek, slid his hands into her hair. "You're everything I've ever wanted, Charlie." He planted kisses along her throat to where her pulse pounded. "Let me love you." He nipped at the thundering beat in her neck. "Let me love you." The words sank into her, healing some gaping wound, and he repeated it like a mantra.

A demand.

A call from his soul to hers.

One she could no longer ignore, no longer refuse. Need unfurled inside her. A deep ache entangled with a much deeper longing to be with him in every way. To be his.

Warmth blossomed low in her belly, radiating through her.

His mouth turned insistent. Hungry. The kiss was

long and wild. She glided her hands down his broad back and skimmed up again, taking his shirt with them. Her deft fingers undid the button on his jeans and lowered his zipper.

In a blink, he was off the bed, on his feet, and he made quick work of getting his jeans and boxer briefs off, tossing them to the floor.

Her jaw went slack at the sight of Aiden in all his naked glory. She'd never tire of seeing him, touching him, kissing this beautiful man, who, beyond reason and despite her numerous flaws, still loved her, wanted her.

Sitting up, she reached for him. He dropped back to the bed and shifted her onto his lap as he sat so she straddled him. She let her towel fall to the side, baring herself to his ardent gaze. He cupped her breast, thumbing the stiff peak as he watched her with a smoldering intensity.

Moaning under his touch, she took the hard, thick length of him in her hand. "I've wanted this for so long. To make love to you," she said, rocking against him. Dampness flooded the space between her legs, anticipation racing under her skin.

"You have no idea. I've wanted you since the day we met." His hand slid over her ribs, down her belly and lower to the apex of her thighs. "Knew we were inevitable." He groaned as he stroked between her folds, making her slick with desire.

As if he'd been studying her, preparing for this moment, he teased with expert fingers, used just the right amount of pressure, which sent an exquisite jolt of pleasure that left her throbbing with need for him.

The inevitability of their commingling, this communion shook her to the core.

Dropping his head to her breast, he sucked hard at a nipple, driving her crazy.

"Aiden." She made a tortured sound of pleading that she'd never imagined possible.

"Patience. You've rushed in the past with others," he said, proving once again how well he knew her. "Not with me. Not the first time, anyway. I need to savor this. You."

"Don't you want to devour me?"

"I intend to. Slowly. For hours." He kissed her with such fierce tenderness that a colony of butterflies took flight inside her on wings of fire.

She'd never been so aroused, so eager, felt so connected to another person.

Charlie didn't think he could get her any more excited or ready, but she couldn't have been more wrong. Exercising inhuman willpower, he made good on his promise. Savored her slowly. He explored every inch of her body from her scalp to the soles of her feet. Licked, tasted, nibbled and sucked, taking her to the brink with his clever tongue, only to deny her the ultimate gratification. Layered pleasure, letting it build and tighten, finally giving her a blinding climax with his head nuzzled between her thighs and his mouth on her.

Screaming his name, she shattered with the most uninhibited release of her life. Sensation thrummed along every nerve. But this wasn't her, wild and begging, writhing and loud.

Two could play the teasing game. It wasn't until she took him in her mouth and gifted him with a similar torture that he tossed her onto her back, flattening her against the mattress, and fully covered her in a motion of unparalleled grace.

She spread her legs wider in invitation.

Sliding his hand up to the back of her neck, he held her tight as he took her mouth and kissed her, deep and hard and wet. His first press into her was long and excruciatingly slow as though it brought him both pleasure and pain.

Which she understood. The friction relieved one kind of ache while making another deepen at the same time.

He rolled over, taking her with him, up into a sitting position. Her legs went around his waist, her hands to his shoulders. He held her hips, guiding her up and down the steely length of him. Pushing up on her knees for leverage, she pulsed with liquid heat, flowed with their building rhythm, matching his hunger and desperation.

"You're so beautiful," he said between ragged breaths. "You're perfect."

They took each other harder and faster, his mouth sensual and sweet, his hands wild and possessive. Her heart brimmed with so much love—with the surety of his, bright as a star—that she cried. Happy tears.

Another shuddering release spilled through her. His arms locked around her waist and he drove her down, grinding roughly until he found his own.

In the past, at this point, once both parties had been physically satisfied, she would've said something callous and goading to establish distance and got the heck out of there.

Instead, when Aiden pulled her down beside him and wrapped his arms around her, she sank into it. Reveled in it.

The sun was fading, and it was nearly dark.

Snuggling with him, she was glad they'd made love

slowly, so she'd always remember every caress, every whispered word of affection, each kiss and exhilarating breath of their first time.

First.

With many, many more to come.

Emotions barraged her. The world had changed.

Even she was different. Sort of. She wanted to be strong enough to handle this, brave enough. Aiden was right. It took courage to love.

"What are we supposed to do now?" she asked as a prickle of anxiety wormed to the surface. "Exchange BFFs bracelets? I guess it should say *lovers*. What does one put when your BFF is your lover?" Charlie pressed her lips together to stop the babbling redirection pouring out of her mouth. She had to be honest with him. Face her fears. "I don't know how to do this, a relationship, and I don't want to mess it up." Her stomach flip-flopped. She wanted it to work between them more than anything, but… "I'm scared."

"I know." He squeezed her arm and rubbed up and down. "We're going to keep doing the same thing that we have been. But we'll do it under one roof, sharing the same bed, only sleeping with each other. No bracelets."

She chuckled, her trepidation easing. "You make it sound so simple."

"Simple, yes. Easy, not always. But don't forget."

"What?"

He kissed her temple and tightened his embrace. "We're the dynamic duo. Together, we can do anything."

Next to Aiden, she felt invincible, like they could conquer the world. Maybe they could make a relationship work. Find happiness one day at a time.

The cell phone on the nightstand buzzed. A text came in.

Aiden reached over and grabbed the phone. He showed her the screen as he opened the message.

An orange jumpsuit wouldn't suit me. What do you want to trade?

"Even if Walsh agrees to give us Albatross, he'll never follow through and make good on it."

"We just have to buy Edgar time. Keep him safe until we can get to him."

Charlie nodded. "We should ask for money, too. To really sell it. Anyone corrupt would."

AS GARCIA ILLEGALLY parked her car in a bus lane on Elk Place, her cell phone rang. She kept the sedan running, took out her mobile and noticed it was the office.

She was about to answer, but she spotted her confidential informant. Her CI abhorred working for the FBI. Most did. After getting busted and charged with drug possession and an intent to distribute, being an informant sounded better than jail, so here they were.

The girl was skittish, but careful. Garcia made their weekly meets as fast as possible to keep her at ease and lessen her exposure.

Whatever McCaffrey wanted would have to wait. She thumbed the reject icon.

The slim brunette pushed through the door of the Tulane University School of Social Work building. They rotated their meeting spot to a place she regularly continued to sell drugs to maintain her cover. The girl came up to the passenger's side of the car, and Garcia rolled down the automatic window.

Colette dug in her voluminous boho tote bag that had a colorful patchwork design and handed over the small six-by-six-inch box through the window. Inside was the special saltshaker that had been designed to match the others at Avido's and had a hidden recording device. The surveillance tool was voice-activated, with up to fifty hours of storage and battery life, and it didn't transmit a signal. Colette kept the saltshaker in the soundproof box in her purse, transporting it to and from the restaurant every day. It was only activated when she served Bill Walsh his lunch.

Garcia gave Colette the replacement device that she'd use for the next seven days.

The exchange was quick and fluid, and to anyone watching, it would look like a drug deal.

"You good?" Garcia asked.

Colette nodded. "Peachy."

Any other response meant something was wrong, like she was under duress or being followed or had been asked to hand over a fake recording. Anything seriously bad.

Colette walked off and Garcia drove in the opposite direction.

Instead of hitting the Windfall tonight, she would go home and start listening to the seven to fourteen hours of audio recording. Walsh was careful. Even in his office he tended to talk around things. But every week she hoped for another nugget while forgoing sleep.

Her phone rang again. This time she answered. "Garcia here."

"It's Jensen," said one of the guys on her surveillance

team. "There's a lot of activity with Walsh. We just lost him. Something is up."

Garcia swore into the phone. "We need to find him. Do you have eyes on the nephew?"

"No. We lost him, too."

Going home and getting to slip off her shoes was out of the question. She was in for a late night, trying to track down Walsh and his sidekick Tommy Guillory.

She slapped the steering wheel. "I'm on my way."

"Also, call the boss. He's looking for you. It's urgent."

Garcia disconnected and dialed Special Agent Mc-Caffrey. "Sorry I couldn't take your call a few minutes ago, sir. What's up?"

"I hope you're sitting down," her boss said.

"As a matter of fact, I am."

"Good. Because you're never going to believe this."

"Well, don't keep me in suspense."

"For starters, you're getting your extra agents tomorrow."

On a Sunday?

"I've got three driving down in the morning from some of the resident field offices in Mississippi," Mc-Caffrey added. "Pascagoula, Hattiesburg and Gulfport."

They were all within a two-hour drive, but that would've taken approval from the director up in Washington, DC, and coordination with the special agent in charge in Mississippi. "How in the world did you swing that?"

"You're going to need heavy backup for a meet tomorrow in Jackson Square at noon."

Chapter Sixteen

The bread truck came to a jerky stop. Big Bill caught hold of one of the steel racks lining the inside to steady himself.

Tommy killed the engine and opened the back doors. Bill climbed out and dusted himself off.

Going from the slightly sweet, yeasty aroma in the truck to the pungent, briny air at the old docks turned his stomach. This far down the river, there weren't any tourists taking in the sights. He took a few deep breaths, letting his nose adjust, and faced the warehouse.

He owned the building and the surrounding land under one of his subsidiaries. The property of each of his illicit businesses, the women and drugs, all fell under a different shell company to disguise the ownership from the feds. They couldn't very well put a place under surveillance and raid it if they didn't know it belonged to him.

Let them watch the Windfall and Avido's to their hearts' content. Didn't matter to him. They were both legit. But it did make traveling somewhat inconvenient at times such as now.

For the next couple of days, he had to steer clear of his house, the restaurant and the casino. He couldn't risk going back until he'd taken out his rage on Edgar and got some retribution.

Fortunately, Bill had a feeder coming in tonight with a new bunch of girls. The small container ship didn't attract as much attention as a larger vessel and it could navigate an older, smaller port. He'd oversee the off-loading of the girls, something Tommy usually took care of, and sleep in one of the passenger cabins once he tired himself out punishing Edgar.

The burner phone they'd used to stay in contact with the hit men from the bayou buzzed in his pocket. A response from those marshals.

It had to be them. They were the only ones in possession of the incriminating information that had been printed, photographed and sent to him. Bill wasn't sure what to make of them yet.

He'd hoped they would've thrown out a figure. Greed he understood, even appreciated. Everyone had a price, and once he'd learned theirs, he could be done with this.

Instead they wanted to trade.

But trade what?

Bill took out the phone and opened the text. For a moment, he was speechless with confusion.

Edgar Plinski. Alive. Unharmed. Plus $1M guarantees no copies of the drive are made.

What in the hell?

Bill read it again, shaking his head in disbelief. What cockamamie planet were these two marshals from? Was this some kind of joke?

Edgar could send him to prison just the same as the information on that flash drive.

Bill furiously typed back.

I need Plinski AND the contents of the drive. Name a new price $.

It took seconds for the phone to chime.

$2M + EDGAR PLINSKI. He's stayed quiet about you this long. We'll get him to keep his mouth shut. We need him to clear our names.

Grinding his molars, Bill kicked the truck tire. Another new message flashed. He stared at the screen.

Nonnegotiable!

Bill growled and shoved the phone back in his pocket.

Removing the delivery jacket and hat, Tommy asked, "What do they want, Uncle Bill?"

"The sun and the moon." They might as well ask for all the stars in the damn sky.

"Huh? What are you talking about?"

Bill shook his head at the kid. "They want," he said slowly, "what they can't have."

Why couldn't they ask for new identities? Help getting out of the country. Something reasonable.

Tommy hustled ahead of him, grabbed the door to the cavernous warehouse that was little more than a gutted-out shell and held it open.

Inside, Devlin and his crew were waiting. Along with a handful of Bill's guys, who'd keep watch over Edgar

Plinski, doling out pain every hour on the hour once Bill was finished having his fun and he gave Tommy a go at him.

But he didn't see the traitor. "Where's that piece of filth?"

Devlin gestured to the van parked a few feet away. "You get the package once we've been paid."

"I'd like to throw in an extra hundred." *Grand* was implied. Devlin didn't get out of bed and put on his outlaw hat for less than ten thousand.

"What for?" Devlin asked.

"To kill those marshals." Bill's men were muscle, good for run-of-the-mill protection and breaking kneecaps. This problem required a shrewd, ruthless predator.

"I need to find them first," Devlin said. "But don't worry. I will."

"No need to find them. They're going to come to me." Bill stuffed his hands in his pants pockets and rocked back on his heels, still fuming. "They texted. They want to trade. The flash drive for Edgar. Alive and unharmed so he can clear their names."

Devlin roared with dark laughter. The sound was spooky enough to give Satan himself the chills. "That's rich."

"Yes. It is. But not the least bit funny."

A smile ghosted across Devlin's lips as he rubbed the back of his head. "Those two have got a lot of grit."

"You almost sound as if you admire them," Bill said, disgusted.

"My father was a hunter. He taught me how to be a great one. To track something to the ends of the earth and kill it. First rule I learned was to respect dangerous things."

Bill huffed. He knew two plus two equaled four. Hell yeah, they were dangerous. That was why he wanted them dead. Respect wasn't a necessary part of his equation.

"I'd kill them for free," Devlin said. "For the sport of it. For payback. But we'll take the extra to fill our captain's pockets."

Their police chief was as crooked as they came. Loved being in front of the camera on the news, spinning manure into glitter, portraying his golden cops as shining examples.

Bill pulled out his other phone and made the call for the wire transfer. Three million six hundred thousand dollars.

"We're good," Tate said to Devlin a minute later, confirming receipt of the money.

Devlin nodded. "Give the man his package."

Tate opened the van door, hauled Edgar Plinski out onto his feet and dragged him over.

Pure satisfaction rushed through Bill's veins. Once the traitor was in front of him, he ripped off the duct tape from his mouth, hoping it hurt. "I'm going to enjoy hearing you scream."

Edgar yelled and howled like a man in agony. Sweat and grime covered his reddening face. "I'll scream all you want. Please, Bill. Don't do this."

"You shouldn't have killed her." *Poor Irene.*

"It was an accident," Edgar said. "I—I loved her. Wanted her to go with me. But she tried to call you and I had to stop her. I didn't mean to kill her. I only hit her once."

Once across the back of her head with a solid bronze

sculpture. Cracked her skull wide open and let her bleed to death.

That was the reason Edgar hadn't turned over evidence on Bill. If the FBI had arrested Bill, he would've told them about Irene's murder and Edgar's immunity would've been null and void. They would've been in prison together. Bill preferred to get his revenge as a free man.

"I've got a long list of things I'm going to do to you. Ways to make you suffer," Bill said. Then he thought about those marshals. *Alive. Unharmed.* "Damn it," Bill hissed and turned to Devlin. "They're going to ask me for proof that he's okay before they meet with me." They'd be fools not to. "But I've waited too long to put off making this one pay," he said, stabbing a finger in Edgar's direction.

"He just needs to *look* okay," Devlin said. "Plenty of options to bring him pain."

"Such as?" Everything Bill had planned was meant to scar and maim.

"Pull out some teeth. Start with the back ones. Rip off toenails. You could do waterboarding, one of my personal favorites. Or insects in a confinement box."

Edgar trembled, shaking his head, mouthing "No, no," dissolving into a pathetic heap as tears streamed down his face.

Good thing Bill had Devlin at his disposal to give him ideas. The man was a sadistic monster of the sickest kind.

"See. Plenty of options," Devlin said cheerfully. "Once we take care of the marshals, then you can really have at it with Edgar."

Grinning, Bill typed a response on the burner phone.

Let's trade. Midnight. Location to follow.

Then he hit Send on the text.

"Tommy," Bill said. "Make a list of the stuff we're going to need. I want to do it all, beginning with a pair of pliers."

Edgar started screaming again and Bill couldn't think of any sound in the world that had ever brought him more pleasure.

We say when. We say where. Or no deal.

Aiden sent the message and shut off the phone. The one thing they had to maintain control over was the rendezvous.

While eating the home-cooked dinner Henri had prepared for them, they sat on the bed in front of the laptop, strategizing their next step. Aiden had already got dressed to go down and get the food, sparing the older lady a trek up the steep flight.

"I think we should give Walsh a location for a fake meet," Charlie said. Wearing his long-sleeve button-up with the front open and revealing a tempting amount of skin, she shifted into a cross-legged position. "Catch them off guard early. Take the fight to them."

"But how? We don't know where they're holding Albatross."

"They're going to have him someplace Walsh completely controls. Somewhere contained, with no danger of him being seen. Not the casino and not the restaurant. His home is out of the question since the feds are watching him. Didn't you mention seeing deeds for other properties?"

"Yeah." Aiden brought up several documents that he'd pored over the night before. "Walsh is in some nasty business. Human trafficking, forcing the women to work in brothels, and he also has his hands in drugs. There are four properties that he's hiding under shell companies. Two are small apartment buildings, one- and two-bedroom units. All appear to be *leased*, but according to this, money is being laundered through there. I assume he's using those apartments for prostitution. If they're active, with a lot of traffic flowing in and out, Albatross won't be there."

"What about the other places?" Charlie finished her crawfish étouffée, scraping the plate clean with her fork.

It was a testament to Henri's cooking. Junior hadn't exaggerated about her culinary skills.

"There's an old processing plant in Metairie and a warehouse down by the docks. No documentation showing any income flowing through either."

"You think Walsh might be holding Albatross at one of those sites?"

"It's possible."

Charlie took a closer look at the paperwork. "We'll have to check them out to narrow it down."

"What you're proposing would require a lot of recon for just the two of us." Aiden ate the last spoonful of his dinner. "We might have to watch one location for a day or longer to be sure that Albatross is there, and we have multiple sites to cover. What if Devlin is holding him for Walsh somewhere else? Even if we did find him, we'd be seriously outnumbered and we're talking about the potential for a lot of bloodshed."

"That's a risk no matter what. I think we have to take the chance."

"If we hit them on their turf, even with the element of surprise, they'll have the advantage. They could use smoke against us again. We can't defeat thermal scopes or use flash bangs in return. We're operating on the shoestring budget and limited resources of street vigilantes."

Resting back on the wood headboard, she sighed. "The only other option is to set a legitimate meet in a public place, but civilians could get hurt. They could be used as human shields. If there's going to be loss of life, I'd prefer it to be the bad guys. We bought Albatross time. Walsh might still hurt him, but he'll be alive. We can do the recon."

Aiden shook his head. Albatross was worth three times more alive just so that he could be tortured. Walsh had a vendetta that he wasn't going to let slide. The odds of Eugene walking away uninjured were nil. "Alive, but in what condition after a day or two? In public, we can have the FBI there in advance waiting for him."

Charlie ran her fingers through his hair. "You're an eternal optimist and I love you for it, but we're fugitives. The FBI consider us a threat and are more likely to arrest us or shoot us before we can ensure Albatross is safe. And don't you think Walsh will send flunkies to check out any location we pick? Maybe even Devlin, who'd spot feds a mile away in a park or shopping mall. Walsh will never get out of the car, especially not with Albatross. We need to use the FBI as our final play."

Aiden ran his hands over his face, racking his brain. "There might be another way." He brought up the city of New Orleans on Google Maps. "What if we spend our time looking for the *right* public place, where we have more control over how everything plays out? Limit collateral damage. Terrain is everything."

Terrain and a lack of convergence led to General Custer's defeat. Why not Walsh's?

"Maybe," she said. "As they say, location is everything. It would mean the difference between success and incarceration or death."

"Controlling the terrain is possible, but Walsh has four highly trained SWAT officers working for him, plus however many thugs. We'd need to even the playing field. Reduce his forces."

Charlie shot him a confident, lopsided grin that was sexy as hell, and all he wanted to do was kiss her, but then he'd want to press down against the mattress, their limbs tangled, and work up a good sweat.

Restraint, he told himself.

"That's where Enzo Romero comes in," Charlie said.

"How so?" Aiden was skeptical about getting a second mobster involved, but Charlie had insisted they might be able to use him.

"The first year I was in a group home as a teenager, I was separated from my sister and surrounded by older, bigger, quite frankly tougher girls. There were two, Tasha and Judy. Both mean. Downright vicious. And they hated each other. Anyway, Tasha took this bracelet that Brit had made for me. I got my butt kicked trying to get it back. One day, someone messed up Judy's bed, went through all her stuff. I told her that it was Tasha."

"Did you do it?"

Charlie shook her head. "No, it was another girl who hated her. But I used it. When Tasha went for Judy, I went and got my bracelet back. We use Enzo to cause trouble that Big Bill can't ignore right before the meet.

If Enzo is already squeezing Bill out, then what we want him to do should be more amusement than a chore."

"Divide and conquer."

"It's the only way to win." She moved their dishes, setting them on the nightstand.

"We need to make a list of places to scout tomorrow morning." He zoomed in on the map. "All within easy walking distance of Jackson Square. Then we should get some sleep. We've got to get up early and tomorrow is going to be a long day."

"Do you want to make that list before or after?" Her mouth spread in a wicked hot smile that instantly heated his blood, igniting something inside him.

He closed the laptop and pulled her closer. "Definitely after."

Chapter Seventeen

Early-morning sun slashed through the opening in the curtains, banishing some of the shadows in the room. Charlie rolled over to find the bed empty, the room quiet and Aiden gone.

The aroma of fresh-brewed coffee wafted through the space. He knew that it was painful for her to operate in the morning without a cup of hot black java.

She ran her palm across the sheet, where he had slept snuggled up against her, and found the spot cold, as though he'd been gone awhile. Much longer than to dash out to get breakfast from Henri. Charlie buried her face in his pillow and smelled him on it.

The scent was comforting and made her ache for the feel of his warmth at her back, the weight of his arm draped over her.

They were neck-deep in a disaster, gambling everything on the choices and actions they made today, and she had never slept better in her entire life than she had last night with Aiden curled around her.

Home. Aiden was her home. Her constant that would never change. No matter how horribly the world fell apart, as long as they were together, she'd be able to deal with it.

Footsteps thudded up the exterior stairs. *Aiden.*

He unlocked the door and swept inside carrying two plates of food covered in aluminum foil. "Good morning. I have breakfast casserole with andouille sausage, eggs and potatoes, and bananas Foster French toast."

"Mmm. It smells delicious. If Aunt Henri keeps this up, we'll never want to leave."

He set the plates on the counter and unwrapped them.

"You were gone a long time." She slipped a shirt on and padded over to him. "Where were you?"

Leaning over, he cupped the back of her head and kissed her gently. Tenderly. "I went to Jackson Square to put things in position while it was still dark, before the FBI sets up."

"You should've woken me. I would've gone with you."

"It only required one of us to take care of it and I wanted to let you sleep."

He was amazing, beautiful, impossibly sweet and so much more than she deserved.

Rising on the balls of her feet, she threw her arm around his neck and kissed him again. "Thanks. But we should stick together."

He poured two cups of coffee and handed her one. "Hurry up and eat, then get dressed. Junior is waiting downstairs to give us a ride so we can check out locations."

She dug into the breakfast and silently sang Henri's praises.

"Which one of us is going to call Enzo and get him in play?" Aiden asked.

"You're better at sweet-talking than I am."

"Sweet won't work on him. I think he needs the way you talk."

Charlie shrugged. "If you think so."

Aiden picked up her jeans and pulled out the business card Enzo had given her with his personal cell number. He dialed using one of the new burners and put the call on speaker.

"Who is this?" Enzo snapped over the line.

"Someone looking to make a deal." She waited, letting his brain wake up and register what she'd said. "If you want what I have on you, then you'll do what I say."

"Listen, sugar. You don't realize who you're speaking to. Nobody tells me what to do."

"Welcome to your new reality. Let's get something straight. I'm not your sugar, your babe or your sweetie." She kept her tone sharp as a switchblade. "I'm your guardian angel. If you're smart enough to want to stay out of prison, you'll do exactly as I say."

A breath of hesitation. "Go on."

"You're going to hit Big Bill where it'll hurt. His brothels. Where he processes his drugs. You're going to make it loud and ugly so Bill has to take notice. The strike happens at two thirty this afternoon. Don't be early. Don't be late."

"Are you trying to start a war?" Enzo asked. "I haven't been sanctioned to take that kind of action."

"Better to beg forgiveness than ask permission. Two thirty. Do this and Bill will no longer be a factor in New Orleans."

THE BELLS OF the St. Louis Cathedral finished clanging, marking the hour. Noon.

With a red hat on and matching T-shirt, Garcia stood

in Jackson Square next to the tree marked on the post-card. It had multiple trunks and wasn't much taller than her five feet ten inches. The offbeat pulse of the French Quarter vibrated around the square.

Adrenaline was the only thing keeping her upright. She was exhausted from spending the night searching for Big Bill Walsh and Tommy Guillory, reviewing security footage of the casino and cross-referencing it with CCTV coverage. She'd only discerned that Walsh had sneaked out in the back of one of the delivery trucks at the casino. The normal schedule had been changed. Deliveries had been deliberately stacked to occur at the same time. The chaos had been too much for two agents to properly monitor.

Walsh and Guillory had slipped through their fingers. They were up to something and it wasn't good. She knew it deep down.

Every chance she had, she'd slogged through more of the audio recording from the restaurant, but there were four more hours to go and she still had no idea where Big Bill was squirreled away.

Garcia scanned her surroundings. Her agents had been in place, rotating positions for the past two hours in various disguises. A homeless man, shuffling around the square. A psychic seated at a small card table on the fringe. Jensen and the agent from Hattiesburg were camped out on a bench fifty feet away, pretending to be a couple, chatting and drinking coffee. The one from Pascagoula pushed a baby stroller with a doll inside and the other from Gulfport was dressed as a jogger, earbuds in, hanging around the vicinity.

A shiver slid down her spine and she sensed she

was being watched. And not by one of her own. That spark of awareness every woman got when unwanted eyes were on her.

It was Aiden Yazzie and Charlotte Killinger. Garcia sensed it in her bones.

Their prints came back first thing this morning with a positive ID on both, and she'd picked up the alert notification that had gone through the FQ Task Force app, placing them in this area yesterday afternoon. None of it was coincidence.

Dirty marshals on the lam contacting the FBI was a first. Maybe they wanted to work out a plea deal in exchange for the evidence they had. Better to make arrangements to be taken into custody unharmed than catch an accidental bullet on the run.

Garcia and her people were prepared to apprehend them without incident. She kept her head on a swivel, surveying the area.

They were out there somewhere and could be in a dozen different places blending in. The Washington Artillery Park. St. Louis Cathedral. Watching from a shop on St. Ann Street or St. Peter.

Garcia glanced at her watch. Two minutes past noon.

A cell phone rang, but it wasn't hers. The ringtone was the song "Bad Boys" by Inner Circle. Loud and close and designed to draw attention.

She followed the sound, tracking it to the palm tree with a cluster of trunks that had been circled on the postcard. The ringing cell phone had been duct-taped to the inner side of one of the trunks in the bunch near the fronds. She hopped up and ripped it off.

There was a flash drive taped to the phone.

She separated the drive and answered. "This is Assistant Special Agent in Charge Ava Garcia."

"I take it you know who I am," a smooth male voice said.

"You're Aiden Yazzie." She looked around, trying to pinpoint him or Killinger. "You know, this conversation would be easier to have face-to-face."

"I can see *your* face," he said in a friendly, conversational tone. "Do you have the drive?"

"I do. It would be best if you came out now, with your hands above your head. I promise no harm will come to either of you as long as you don't resist arrest."

"We're not turning ourselves in. Not until we've rescued the witness we lost."

Edgar Plinski. "You were the ones who gunned down fellow law enforcement officers and allowed Albatross to be taken." After reading the despicable details of the case, she'd found out the witness's code name.

"We're innocent," he said. "We were set up by the crew who ambushed us. They're crooked NOPD SWAT officers out of the Fifth District, hired by Bill Walsh. They're led by Frank Devlin."

Garcia knew the name. She'd suspected Devlin was dirty for a while, and when he turned out to be the only eyewitness accusing Yazzie and Killinger, it had struck her as fishy. Too convenient.

"If you dig," Yazzie said, "you'll find that Devlin and three other owners of The Merry Men bar were out of town Friday."

The FBI's top criminal investigative priority was public corruption. Any violations of federal law by public officials at the federal, state and local levels of government. She'd heard rumors about rotten apples in the

Fifth District reaching the highest branches of power, but no one had been able to prove anything. One dead end after another. Sometimes literally, with witnesses having accidents or disappearing.

However, a fugitive's say-so wasn't going to cut the mustard. Even if Devlin and his buddies had been out of town, it wasn't proof. It was circumstantial at best.

"We've promised Walsh that he can have the flash drive you're holding," Yazzie said, "in exchange for giving us back Albatross, alive and unharmed."

Garcia scoffed. "And how do you see that playing out?"

"I foresee you using the information on the drive to put away Walsh and Enzo Romero. That evidence along with more has been sent to the DOJ. At the meet, Walsh will have his men try to kill us."

"What's to stop them from doing that?"

"Hopefully, you."

"Come again?"

"We're asking for your help. Call it interagency cooperation. The rendezvous will take place at three o'clock. In a public place that's less than one mile from where you're standing."

The FBI had achieved great success in combating corruption thanks in large part to working with other agencies on a federal, state, local and tribal law enforcement level, including the Department of Justice and by extension the US Marshals Service, but what Yazzie proposed was well outside of legal bounds.

"Give me the location now," Garcia said.

"I can't do that."

"Can't or won't?"

"Both."

Provided he was telling the truth, her people would be able to respond quickly if the location was less than a mile away, but she preferred going in early ahead of time. "If you truly want to cooperate with the FBI, you wouldn't stonewall. Full disclosure."

"Proof of our cooperation is on the flash drive you're holding."

"Why not share the site of the meet?"

"I'll give you six reasons. The vagrant, the two sitting on the bench chitchatting like they're a couple, the tarot reader in blue with sunglasses, jogger wearing track pants, woman pushing a stroller on your left. All six are yours. If I tell you where, you'll scare off Walsh. He and Devlin will spot your agents."

"Then how am I supposed to help you?"

"Keep the phone in your hand close. We'll call again from a different number when the time is right."

The call ended.

Slapping the flip phone closed, Garcia grunted in frustration and slid it into her pocket.

Jensen stared at her, waiting. When she shook her head that the marshals turning themselves in was a no-go, he came over. "Anything useful?"

"Maybe." *Hopefully.* "According to them, Walsh has Albatross. They claim they're innocent and are meeting Walsh to get their witness back. Supposedly this drive," she said, holding it up, "has everything we need to put away Walsh *and* Romero."

"Why would they give it to you when they could use it as leverage?"

Leverage? Hell, it was probably worth millions. "They say they're innocent. That they were set up by the people who kidnapped Albatross."

"Do they know who?"

"Aiden Yazzie swears it was Frank Devlin and several other SWAT officers."

Jensen's brow furrowed and he looked down like
something had occurred to him. "Devlin was at Avido's
yesterday afternoon."

"What?" Garcia rocked back on her heels. "Why didn't
you tell me?"

"He was there during regular business hours. It could've
been just to eat, and once Walsh disappeared, finding him
was our only focus."

Didn't it occur to Jensen that the two incidents could've
been related?

If what Yazzie had told her was true, Devlin probably
went to Avido's to coordinate payment and the drop-off
of Albatross.

Garcia shoved the flash drive in Jensen's hand. "Have
everyone stay close by for the next couple of hours and I
want you to verify the contents of the drive." She turned
and took off.

"Where are you going?" he called after her.

"To check the end of the recording from Avido's. See
if we got the conversation."

Chapter Eighteen

After Bill had waited twenty-one hours, the burner phone on his side table in the small passenger cabin buzzed.

Audubon Aquarium. Send a picture of Edgar Plinski standing in front of the aquarium sign, Canal Street side, by three o'clock, or the deal is off. No Devlin.

Bill chuckled. The gumption of those marshals to think they could dictate to him. Bill would be crazy not to show up with Devlin, the most merciless monster on his payroll, to finish this.

With only thirty minutes to be at the aquarium, they needed to get going.

Stretching, he held his hands up and stared at the bloodstains under his nails. He should've worn gloves before he ripped out a few of Edgar's teeth.

Out of all the ways he'd tortured Edgar, for hours, none had brought Bill more than a modicum of the satisfaction that he sought.

He sighed but was comforted by the knowledge that soon the marshals would be dead, and Edgar would be his to do with as Bill pleased.

Then he'd work through his pain and grief with his fists.

Someone pounded on his cabin door. "Uncle Bill! Open up!"

Bill threw on his suit jacket, slicked back his hair and hit the lever, opening the door. "What is it?"

"Enzo. He's making a play."

"For the brothels?"

"No. For everything! His men are at both the apartment buildings, rounding up the girls, kicking out the johns, taking the money, and they're also at the processing plant. He's stealing our dope."

Had the whole world gone mad? An hour ago, Bill had been on the precipice of ruling New Orleans again. Now he was being threatened on all fronts.

"We've got to get over there and stop him," Tommy said.

"I can't. I have to head out for the meet." Bill left his room and walked with Tommy down the narrow corridor. "If I'm not there, I'll lose the drive."

"You're losing everything else right this minute."

Bill cursed the bad timing of things. Enzo must've noticed that he wasn't around and decided it was the perfect time to make his move. Damn vulture.

"You go handle it, Tommy." Bill knocked on Devlin's door and said, "It's time. We've got twenty-seven minutes. Grab Edgar and let's go."

"You want me to handle it?" Tommy asked, following Bill as he pushed through the outer door into the sunlight.

"Yeah, you. This will all be yours someday. You've got just as much of a stake in it as I do, and I trust you to deal with it." He clasped his nephew's shoulder and that seemed to calm him. "Take the boys with you."

"Are you sure? Who's gonna cover your back?"

"I've got Devlin and his crew. They're more than enough. After we're finished, I'll come help you get back what's ours."

WEARING THEIR WIGS and sunglasses, Charlie and Aiden leisurely finished their snack at the eatery, blending in. Once done, they strolled from the Café du Monde, where they'd observed Special Agent Garcia during their phone call, down by the river toward the Audubon Aquarium. They were both armed: tactical knives, suppressed firearms, and her telescoping baton was hooked to her belt loop and covered by her button-up shirt that she wore open over her tee.

If they could use nonlethal means, they would. Limiting collateral damage was a huge concern. They'd do everything in their power to protect innocent lives.

As they crossed through a playground, laughter from the kids playing there filled the air. Without meaning to, she looked over at the children whooshing down a slide.

She thought of the sacrifice Aiden was making by choosing to be with her.

The guilt she'd been trying so damn hard to ignore sank into her chest, an ache flaring sudden and sharp behind her breastbone.

But she had to shift focus, stay on target. On the mission. On getting Albatross back from those crooked cops who'd ambushed them, taken out their tires, sprayed paint on the windows, faked a bomb, used smoke and thermal scopes.

That fired her up, pushing the sadness aside.

Passing the sandbox, Charlie bent down, scooped up two healthy palmfuls of grains and put them into her pocket.

"What's that for?" Aiden asked, hiking the backpack up on his shoulder.

"To fight dirty." If given the chance. "Like them," she said, anger resonating in her voice.

"Don't worry. We're going to give them a dose of their own medicine."

They had a plan to do precisely that.

They entered the aquarium flashing the handstamp they'd received earlier when they'd paid and scoped out the place. Once again, the backpack hadn't been searched. Good thing, too, because Aiden had more than duct tape inside.

The main exhibits were emptying, as parents with kids and others were making their way to the Entergy Giant Screen Theater. The IMAX theater was connected to and run by the aquarium but had a separate entrance outside.

The 3D larger-than-life movies explored nature, shown with the most advanced motion picture technology, and were a huge draw. They timed the meet to coincide around a show to reduce the number of civilians that would be inside the aquarium.

Aiden took her by the hand, leading her into the glass underwater tunnel of the Great Mayan Reef, which was set off to the side. No one entering the aquarium could see them. Surrounded by water that cast an azure glow over them and sea creatures from moray eels to stingrays swimming by, he backed her up against the glass wall and pressed his palm to her face. "Find a discreet spot outside to keep watch. I'll go set up and prepare upstairs."

The Amazon Rainforest Exhibit on the second floor was the best site to face Walsh. It was a contained area that was currently closed for repairs, and there were two ways to access it. One was farther down the corridor, beyond the Mayan Reef and to the stairs. The other, more obvious, route was through the main section of the aquarium to the stairs that led to the upper-floor exhibits.

"I don't like separating," Charlie said.

"Devlin might come. He'll use guerrilla tactics. If you keep watch outside, you can let me know who's headed my way."

"If I see Devlin—"

"Stay away from him."

She'd do whatever was necessary to cover Aiden's back. If Devlin showed, he'd have to go through her first before she gave him an opportunity to get the drop on her man. *Hers.*

"Devlin is dangerous," Aiden said, probably reading the bullheaded look in her eyes.

"So am I. You can't take on an entire team alone. We're partners. Don't try and sideline me because I'm a woman or because you love me. We only win if we do it together."

Reluctantly, he said, "All right. But if you see Devlin, don't follow him. Come straight to the exhibit. We'll deal with him together."

She put her palm to his chest, stared into his deep brown eyes, finding her center. "Do you have any bad feelings?"

He nodded, his lips pressing tight like he didn't want to say more.

She wasn't going to push him. "Be careful."

"Always. You, too."

Charlie had no clue what was going to transpire once Walsh arrived in the next few minutes, but she'd promised herself to tell Aiden, every single day, what he meant to her. "I love you."

He lowered his head and kissed her, hard, quick. "See you soon." With that, he was off.

Taken aback, Charlie snatched his wrist and pulled him into the dim blue light. "Hey, Mr. Romantic, aren't you going to say it back?" Weren't couples supposed to do that? Exchange mushy sentiments before separating and running into danger.

"After," he said. The single, steely word was his promise to her that they'd get through this, that this wasn't their last chance to share what was in their hearts.

Oddly enough, it filled her with hope. "After." Another peck on the lips, and she let him leave.

She watched him take the entrance to the Rainforest Exhibit through the Mayan Reef and head past the sign that read Closed for Repairs.

Outside, she found a spot on a bench under a large shade tree, facing the river. The position gave her lines of sight to anyone approaching the entrance from the south or north and was partially concealed by a closed kiosk.

She put in her wireless earpiece. "One, two, can you hear me?" she said, doing a comms check.

"Loud and clear," Aiden responded. "I'm all set up. It's quiet in here. I think they moved the birds for whatever maintenance they're doing. Fish are still in the tank. Hey, did you know that a school of piranha can strip the flesh from a one-hundred-pound capybara in under a minute using razor-sharp teeth?"

"No, and neither did you until you read that on a sign."

Useless fact, but the viciousness made Charlie think she needed that same ferocious survival instinct.

She'd never had anything in her life as precious as Aiden's love. They had a chance at a future together, and she was going to fight like hell to keep it.

They needed a four-man team for this. Something Devlin had and they lacked. Hopefully, Enzo was doing his part. If an army of thugs showed up at the aquarium, they'd have to retreat and regroup.

At three o'clock sharp, a text came in. Charlie opened the attachment, finding a picture of Edgar Plinski at the south side of the aquarium, as they'd instructed.

Edgar was pale, with horror-filled eyes and puffy cheeks, looking as if he was on the verge of a breakdown. They must have put him through the wringer.

Charlie sent the exact location for the meet.

Amazon Rainforest Exhibit. Second level.

A man she recognized from Devlin's group photo approached from the east, alone, and went inside.

"Albatross is here, and a scout just entered, checking the place out. One of Devlin's."

"Roger," Aiden said. "I'll contact Garcia. Tell her to get over here ASAP."

Devlin's scout would do a thorough sweep, making sure it was clear of feds and cops, and that nothing suspicious stood out.

By the time Garcia arrived, the meet would be underway, and it'd be too late.

The scout must've been satisfied, because a few minutes later, another goon appeared with his hand locked on Edgar's arm, dragging him toward the entrance.

Walsh followed at least ten paces behind them, carrying a briefcase and looking way too cocky, like this scenario was a foregone conclusion for him.

"Two SWAT operators and Albatross and Walsh are headed your way."

"Got it," Aiden said. "Don't rush in. Play it cool. Make sure there are no surprises coming up on my six."

"Okay." Tension rippled through Charlie, but she forced herself to appear relaxed, like a tourist enjoying the day.

Then everything changed.

From the corner of her eye, she saw them. Not a squad of armed thugs. Something worse.

Devlin and one of his buddies, lean and mean with a goatee, rounded the corner from the north side in a furious stride. They were out for blood.

She swore under her breath.

Stopping at the employee entrance, Devlin rang the bell and pounded on the door with a fist. A staff member opened the door.

Devlin flashed his badge, shoved the kid aside and bulldozed his way in along with the other guy.

A rush of dread, cold as liquid nitrogen, shot through her. "They're inside," Charlie said. "Devlin and another."

"Wait for Garcia. She's mobilizing. She'll be there in ten minutes. Stay outside."

Panic flipped to fury. Like hell she'd sit outside while they killed Aiden.

She had one advantage. With the wig, they didn't know what she looked like. She could get close and do damage before they even realized it was her.

"You could be dead in ten minutes. I'm going after Devlin."

She'd do anything to protect Aiden, and everything in her power to keep them both alive.

AN EERIE SPARK of awareness had trickled down Aiden's spine the minute he'd sent the text to Walsh about meeting at the aquarium. Someone was going to die today.

Now Charlie was rushing off to handle Devlin and one of his SWAT buddies alone.

And there wasn't a damn thing he could do about it. His chest squeezed with stark fear.

Impulsive, hotheaded, gorgeous woman! You better stay alive and not get hurt.

They'd waited too long, fought too hard, to lose each other.

She was smart. A fighter. A dirty fighter. Devlin had probably better watch out, he told himself, seeking a shred of solace.

One of the crooked cops wearing a ball cap entered the exhibit, scanning the area that was created to resemble the rainforest.

Aiden kicked the empty backpack at his feet out of his way.

Once the cop spotted Aiden standing on the Tree-Top Loop, a wooden bridge that connected two canopies with a small covered pavilion at one end, the cop moved to the bottom of the left staircase and stopped.

The position in the Tree-Top Loop gave Aiden enough camouflage from the pavilion to prevent him from being an easy target and a bird's-eye view of the entire exhibit, along with both exits.

Walsh sauntered in carrying a briefcase, with a smug smile on his face. Behind him Albatross shuffled in, his head hung low.

The other dirty SWAT officer, who had outdated sideburns that Elvis wanted back, held a gun pressed to Edgar's temple.

"Here he is as promised, and the money." Walsh held up the briefcase and opened it, revealing bundles of cash. "Where's the flash drive?"

"Are you all right?" Aiden asked Edgar. "Did they hurt you?"

"He's walking and talking," Walsh said. "So he's fine."

Sweat trickled down the side of Aiden's face from the steamy jungle atmosphere as he raised an eyebrow. "Well, I haven't heard the talking part yet." For all he knew, they'd cut out the man's tongue.

"Tell him." Walsh poked Edgar in the cheek.

Wincing, Edgar recoiled. "I'm fine." His voice was low and hoarse, like he'd been screaming and lost it.

"I want a closer look at him before any exchange. Bring him up here." Aiden waved them up the right set of stairs.

As Edgar limped up the steps with Sideburns behind him, the other man set a foot on the left staircase.

"No." Aiden drew the suppressed Beretta he'd stolen from Devlin and pointed it at him. "You and Walsh stay there. Just them."

Edgar and Sideburns continued walking. The others stayed put.

Aiden backed up, drawing them in to where he wanted, without the gunman feeling crowded, threatened. Shifting to the side, Aiden guided them to move clockwise, ninety degrees. Right where the proverbial X marked the spot.

Sideburns held the back of Edgar's shirt collar with one hand and leveled the gun at his head with the other.

Looking over Edgar, Aiden noticed his eyes were bloodshot and swollen, and he kept swallowing in a weird way, like his mouth was sore. Hundreds of tiny red marks covered his face, throat, hands.

Were those bug bites?

Aiden had a plan to keep the conversation going until Garcia arrived. Edgar's current state was the perfect thing to pursue and draw things out, but every second he wasted stalling was one more second that Devlin had to kill Charlie.

"Where's the flash drive?" Walsh asked.

In his peripheral vision, Aiden caught the one wearing the ball cap slip his gun from his holster and creep up the left staircase, one slow step after another.

"Set the briefcase on the ground," Aiden said, tracking the progress of the one moving. By the time Walsh did as he was told, the other man reached the midway point on the stairs.

Precisely where Aiden wanted.

They were always going to try to close in around him. No warnings or threats were going to stop it, only delay it. So he had to prepare for the inevitable.

With the lush jungle environment, leafy tropical plants and verdant vegetation, it was easy to miss all the items that Aiden had hidden.

He let the guy take one more step. Then Aiden pulled the Smith & Wesson from his waistband with his left hand, aimed at the booby trap and pulled the trigger.

The portable fire extinguisher taped to a pole and concealed with palm fronds exploded in the guy's face. He shrieked and slipped backward down the stairs.

Aiden dropped to one knee—anticipating Sideburns would refocus the barrel of his gun away from Edgar's head toward the threat—and took aim in his direction. Edgar instinctively cowered, his hands covering his head, arms in front of his face as Aiden fired again.

With a loud *pop*, a second extinguisher exploded, sending a cloud of dry white chemicals bursting through the air around the pavilion.

Sideburns screamed, throwing an arm up to cover his face.

Aiden coughed from the particles in the air but had turned away to avoid getting any in his eyes. He reached out and pulled Edgar to the ground, getting him out of the way, and shoved him into the corner.

A bullet hit a nearby wooden post. Walsh was firing at them.

"Stay down, here," Aiden said to Edgar. Then he jumped up and threw a side kick into Sideburns's chest.

The blow drove the thug backward, the momentum carrying him over the rail of the pavilion into the piranha tank below.

Aiden launched himself down the right staircase, spraying a volley of suppressive fire from the 9 mm with the silencer.

If Walsh had gone left toward the stairs leading to the Mayan Reef, he would've got away without a scratch on him. Instead he ran in the direction in which he'd come, back toward the other exhibits on the second floor.

Aiden aimed and fired. Not at Walsh. And he was out of fire extinguishers. His bullet hit a cluster of paint ball grenades. The yellow liquid color sprayed in multiple directions, making the floor slick.

He could always count on Charlie to get creative in a pinch.

Running, Walsh couldn't get any traction in his fancy shoes and slipped around like he was trying to walk on ice.

Aiden punched him in the face, knocking Walsh to his butt, and kicked the gun from his hand.

A bullet struck a tree beside Aiden's head. The one in the ball cap had recovered, but the chemicals from the extinguisher had messed up his eyes. His aim was off.

Aiden returned fire.

The guy ducked and hit the stairs, going for Edgar. Heavy footfalls pounded up the right staircase, followed by more gunfire.

Leaping into action, Aiden rounded the corner and saw Edgar making a run for it across the wooden bridge and down the steps on the left side of the room. Aiden popped off a round, clipping the gunman in the leg.

The man dropped onto the stairs.

Staying on him, Aiden bounded up the steps, but the guy rolled onto his back. At that distance, a blind man could've shot him.

Aiden darted to the side at the right moment, avoiding a hot slug to the chest. He stilled and controlled the squeeze of the trigger. One shot to the wrist, forcing the man's fingers to open and drop the weapon. The guy howled, clutching his wounded arm.

Pulling out a zip tie, Aiden flipped the guy onto his stomach.

Edgar kept going. Darting down below, he scooped up the briefcase full of cash and took off running.

"Wait, Edgar!" Aiden called as he disappeared down the stairs toward the Mayan Reef.

Walsh was up on his feet, gun back in his hand, and hot on Edgar's heels.

Aiden yanked the man's arms behind his back and got his wrists and ankles restrained with zip ties. Then Aiden was up, on the move, again.

But as he ran down the stairs, he realized he had to make a choice.

Go after Edgar and Walsh. Or find Charlie.

Everything that they'd gone through—running from the law, taking on gangsters, going toe-to-toe with dirty SWAT officers to clear their names—would be in vain if they lost Edgar. Their careers, their future, would go down the drain.

His heart throbbed with immediate resolution. There was no choice.

CHARLIE FINALLY SPOTTED one of Devlin's men in the Gulf of Mexico Exhibit. The area was dimly lit so visitors could clearly see the seventeen-foot-deep, 400,000-gallon tank with sharks and other marine life, and a quarter-scale replica of an offshore oil rig.

The exhibit was stunning and at the same time alarming. Darkness shrouded the corners, black pockets like ominous voids. And there was still no sign of Devlin.

The man with the goatee was headed toward the Great Mayan Reef.

Was Devlin in front of them already, at the Amazon Rainforest Exhibit?

Or was he lurking somewhere behind her?

She took another furtive glance over her shoulder. Nothing but a family strolling toward a different exhibit in the opposite direction. Charlie pulled out her baton. The steel was well-balanced and heavy-duty.

The expandable rod would allow her to make physical contact while giving her a twenty-six-inch buffer zone. That might not be much, but when it came to a 200-pound man throwing a punch, those two feet of safety distance felt like ten.

She squeezed the rod in her hand, keeping her head on a swivel.

Timing the meet to coincide with the movie in the theater next door had worked. The place was fairly empty now compared to this morning, and the darkness seemed to have swelled as the number of people wearing bright-colored clothing dwindled.

The employee entrance opened in the middle of the aquarium. Devlin could be anywhere. She hoped she found him before he got to Aiden.

Goatee spotted something, picking up his pace as he reached into his jacket for his weapon.

With a quick flick of the wrist, the telescoping baton extended to full length. She swooped up behind him and whacked his gun arm twice, stopping him from drawing his weapon.

A couple in the vicinity gasped and ran for the exit.

Then Charlie went for the startled man's legs, hitting him behind the knees, bringing him to the floor. Hard.

He looked up at her, snarling. "You bit—"

Another strike to his face silenced him. She kicked

him to the floor facedown and thrust her knee in the middle of his back.

Setting the baton on the floor, she pulled out zip ties and bound his wrists behind him.

"Charlie, where are you?" Aiden asked over comms.

She went to toggle her earpiece as a shocking blow to her head sent her spinning off the man and the black wig went flying. Charlie crashed into the wall.

A follow-up kick to her gut had her doubled over in pain.

Dazed, she swung out with a fist on pure instinct, but her attacker laid her on the floor with a leg sweep. As she sucked in for air, trying to breathe through the pain, he dropped on top of her, and she stared into Devlin's hateful eyes.

Her blood turned to ice, heartbeat thrumming sickeningly in her ears.

"Thought you could hunt me. That a wig would make you invisible. Like I couldn't draw you out." He cocked his fist, bringing his elbow way back, preparing to hurt her. Hurt her until there was only darkness.

She had to fight, act now. Charlie brought a knee up between his legs hard enough to jolt him forward and threw a punch up into his throat.

Then he was the one gasping.

He rolled off her, and she clambered to her feet.

Staggering away, she needed to get distance from him. She reached into her shirt to draw her weapon when a hand closed around her ankle. He yanked her back with such force that she had to throw out both hands in front of her to break the fall.

He was climbing on her, with her belly to the floor.

Facedown, she wouldn't stand a chance.

Charlie swung her elbow back and up, using the added rotation of her body to drive it hard into the side of Devlin's head. Her bone struck his face. He grunted and his weight lifted.

Without hesitation, she scrambled forward on her hands and knees. Pushed up from the floor to her feet.

Devlin growled. A shuffling sound told her that he was in motion behind her. A bullet bit into the wall near her head.

She bolted for the stairs. Her brain spun. Dread pooled in her stomach. Faster and faster she ran.

"Charlie!" Aiden's panicked voice in her ear reset her senses.

She spotted a sign that said Second Floor: Shark Discovery.

The new shark and stingray touch-pool exhibit was under construction. She grabbed the knob and jerked it. Locked. Her heart felt ready to explode in her chest.

"Don't go there. It's locked," Aiden said.

With a desperate curse, she drew her weapon.

Devlin pounded up the steps. His vile, evil energy was a force in itself, breathing down on her.

She shot the lock and kicked it open. Devlin charged toward her, taking aim. She threw the door wide open, punched holes into the other and ran into the construction zone.

Before she could get her bearings, he was barreling down on her.

She spun and fired but tripped on a cord and missed.

As he raised his gun, she was close enough to grab his right wrist and keep her head out of the line of fire, but he snatched her gun hand, as well.

They wrestled, struggling in a furious whirl to gain

control or to break free. Both squeezing off shots, trying to nail the other with a bullet.

His gun clicked first. Empty.

Two more shots, and hers did the same.

The moment of decision froze between them, and their eyes locked.

One bloody lesson she'd learned in the group home as a teenager—hesitation could be fatal. Letting a fight unfold always gave your opponent the advantage.

She threw a headbutt to his face, slamming her skull down on the bridge of his nose, and nearly broke free of his hold. But he was tough. Unrelenting.

Devlin punched her, a quick jab that sent her to the floor and had blood pooling in her mouth.

Think! She inched away. Determination fired in her blood.

Think, or this man is going to kill you.

She'd never given much thought to dying, had never spent much time wondering what came after. But right then, all she cared about was living and breathing and having a life with Aiden. She wasn't going to let this bastard take that away from her.

He stalked closer, violence etching harsh lines on his face.

Charlie shoved her hand in her pocket and gathered a handful of sand. *Hold*, she told herself. Pulse racing. Breath sawing from her mouth. *Wait for him to get closer.*

He reached down to grab her by the hair, and she threw the sand in his eyes.

Pitching away from her, he wiped at his face with his forearm.

She threw a boot heel to his groin.

Jumping to her feet, she drew the tactical knife from its sheath and lunged for him. The matte black blade slid into the sweet spot—the jugular notch right above the sternum.

A gurgling noise came from Devlin. He stumbled back, dropped to one knee as if still struggling to stand, to keep fighting out of sheer malice, but he toppled to the floor.

His lifeless eyes open. Blood pouring from his dead body on the floor.

She sucked in a deep breath and swallowed hard, her hands shaking. Her heart quivering.

Aiden stormed inside. His gaze fell to Devlin and lifted to her. The heated look in his eyes knocked her back a step. She saw the anger, the worry, the shadows of fear.

In a blink, he had her wrapped in his arms.

Relief rose like the sun inside her. They'd both survived. Together. She held him tight, pressed her cheek to his.

Then she remembered. Pulling away, she asked, "Where's Albatross?"

"He ran with the money. Walsh went after him."

She stared at him, her mouth hanging open. "Why aren't you chasing them?"

He ran his hand over her hair and caressed her jaw. "I had to make sure you were all right."

Shock left her speechless. The depth of his love was staggering. Blinding.

"You'll always come first," he said. "Before duty, before country. Before anything."

With a lump forming in her throat, she slid her hands

up his chest and he enveloped her in his arms. She soaked in his warmth, his comfort. His love.

The distinct sound of helicopter blades cutting through the air outside quieted them.

They ran out of the room.

From the window, they saw a police helicopter hovering in the front of the aquarium.

They exchanged a glance and ran down the stairs, racing to the main entrance.

Beyond the doors, Walsh stood with his arm around Edgar's throat and a gun to his head. A hundred feet away, Special Agent Garcia had her weapon drawn alongside several other agents and had them surrounded.

Aiden took a step toward the doors with his gun raised.

"What are you doing?" Charlie grabbed his arm. "If you go out there, they might shoot you. They think we're fugitives."

Aiden considered what she'd said for a moment, pulled the cell from his pocket and called the burner he'd given Garcia.

What if she didn't answer?

She might not even be able to hear it with the helicopter overhead.

But Garcia patted her pocket and pulled out the phone.

"We're inside the aquarium," Aiden said. "We have a clean shot. But I need you to let us take it." He listened for a minute and hung up. "She's ordering everyone to hold their fire. The shot is ours."

Trepidation rippled through Charlie. It could be a trick, to get them to expose themselves, but Garcia wanted Walsh and to protect Albatross, a witness, as much as they did.

"I'll hold the door," Charlie said. "You take the shot."

Aiden was a better marksman. Not by much, but enough to wound Walsh and save Edgar's life. She couldn't guarantee the same. Shooting to kill was more her style.

They crept up to the entrance, waving back frightened employees, urging them to stay low.

Charlie grabbed a door handle, took a breath to stop nerves from rolling her stomach and waited for Aiden's signal.

With a two-handed grip for increased stability and accuracy, he raised the weapon, lining up his sights.

When he gave a sharp nod, she flung the door open.

Aiden squeezed the trigger once.

The bullet struck Walsh in the shoulder, causing the gun to jerk forward without discharging. Aiden fired again, hitting his hand. The weapon dropped to the ground.

FBI agents swept in and circled the two men.

Charlie and Aiden lowered their guns to the ground and put their hands up behind their heads, assuming the standard position.

Cuffs were slapped on Walsh. "I'm going to tell them!" Walsh said. "About how you murdered my sister. Say goodbye to your immunity. I might be going to prison, but you'll be right there beside me!"

Edgar shuddered as agents took the briefcase and escorted him away.

"You can lower your hands," Garcia said, approaching them. "You've been cleared of charges."

"How?" Charlie and Aiden asked in unison.

"I've got Walsh and Devlin on tape. Devlin admitted to framing you. When I called your San Diego field office to let your boss, Will Draper, know, he informed me that Albatross's wife came out of her coma this morning. She told the police what really happened. Apparently, Draper had marshals providing protection for her around the clock, in case you two decided to...well." She stopped, not voicing the vile implication. "It was a good thing, too. A local cop tried to kill her."

"What?" Charlie asked.

"The cop was Devlin's buddy who'd provided his cover story for being out in San Diego."

Devlin was trying to tie up loose ends, including her and Aiden. Edgar Plinski was saved for last.

"Thank you for contacting our superior," Aiden said. "And for not shooting us."

Garcia smiled. "Glad I could help."

"What's going to happen to Albatross?" Charlie asked.

"We'll keep him safe in custody while we investigate Mr. Walsh's allegations. If they're true, Albatross will lose immunity and be sent to prison."

It made sense that he'd kept quiet about Walsh in order to protect himself from a murder charge.

"When are you going to get Enzo Romero?" Aiden asked.

"We heard he made a big power play today," Garcia said.

Charlie and Aiden exchanged a glance but said nothing.

"Thanks to the information you gave us," Garcia continued, "we're going to get a warrant and bring him in. After I get some rest."

"Thank you again for your help," Charlie said, shaking her hand.

Aiden did likewise. "There are four more inside. The dirty SWAT cops that ambushed us. Two are dead, including Devlin."

Garcia nodded. "This is proof that interagency cooperation works." She stepped past them inside.

"What now?" Charlie asked Aiden.

He circled his arm around her shoulders, and they started walking away from the hubbub of the scene. "Now we go back to our rented room in time for dinner. Henri's serving blue crab gumbo. We shower, make love and talk about my job offer at Camp Beauregard."

Being an instructor someday was always Aiden's goal. She couldn't give him children, but she could make sure he accepted his dream job. No way in the world would she take that away from him.

"There's nothing to talk about," Charlie said. "You're taking the job. End of discussion."

"Not so fast." He kissed her head. "If I take the job, we've got to talk about how to get you out there, too."

"Me?" She looked up at him, confused. "They're not going to make me an instructor and I'm not quitting."

He crushed his mouth down on hers, his palms sliding up and down her body, his strong arms pulling her against him so tightly she could scarcely breathe, and the worries swimming in her head dissolved.

Drawing his lips back, he smiled at her. "Where there's a will, there's a way, and when we're together, anything is possible. Have a little faith. In us."

Epilogue

The sun was setting, taking the natural light with it. Charlie grabbed another box from the back of the portable moving container that had been shipped from San Diego, and strode out into the steamy Louisiana air. The day had been long and hot and muggy, and the air-conditioning in their new house was on the fritz. An HVAC repairman wouldn't be able to come out for two days, and every time she turned around, it seemed like something else in the place had broken.

She'd be happier once the temperature dropped and Aiden came home from the Special Operations Group Tactical Center at Camp Beauregard.

Her new position there as a full-time SOG member assigned to one of the special teams didn't start for another two weeks. But she had a month of unused leave.

This was giving them a chance to settle in and find their baseline before his twelve-hour training days started and she deployed on a mission. Thankfully, Aiden hadn't fed into her worst fears and turned into a Neanderthal, demanding she not go out in the field without him. No, he was the best kind of man, a friend and partner. He trusted her to take care of herself.

Landing her a position so that they could be together

had taken some finagling. Aiden told his supervisor that she was his fiancée, and since he didn't want to be a liar, he had popped the question.

For Charlie, she didn't need a ring or marriage or a piece of paper making things legal. She just needed Aiden. If going the traditional route kept them together, then she wasn't going to argue over a piece of jewelry and signing a license.

A car door slammed, and she spun around on the stairs leading up to the wraparound porch.

Aiden climbed out of his SUV with a bright smile on his face, and every single awful thing about the day melted away. As he hustled over to her, she set the box of dishes down on the porch. He reached out for her and she fell into his arms.

She kissed him, hungry and impatient. Ready to take his clothes off and lose herself in the feel of him. In his breath, the taste of him, the smell of him. While unpacking, she'd thought of nothing but undressing him and christening another room in the house.

To her surprise, she heard a motorcycle drawing closer. A single beam of light sliced through the trees lining the driveway, and a motorcycle coasted around the corner. Not one that was fast enough to race a Ducati, but it sure did look cool. And as bikes went, it was quiet on the gravel driveway. The guy parked behind Aiden's car, eased the kickstand in the down position and killed the engine.

"You didn't tell me we were having company," she said.

"It was a last-minute thing. I tried to call, but you didn't answer."

Her cell phone was in the kitchen on the counter, with music blasting. She must've been in the moving container when he called, and she hadn't thought to check for any missed messages.

The little things didn't come naturally, but Aiden cut her a lot of slack and encouraged her to do the same for herself.

They were in this together and would create rules that suited them. No need to talk of a wedding date until they were both ready. There wasn't even pressure to buy a dog.

But checking her phone for missed calls would have to be added to the list of rules.

The man took off his helmet and raked a hand through close-cropped light brown hair.

Clean-shaven with a streamlined, muscular physique and tattoos running the length of his arms, he had a thuggish vibe that spelled trouble. In Charlie's previous life, he would've been the perfect type for a one-night stand.

"Charlie, this is Horatio Haas. He works on one of the special teams."

"Please, call me Dutch," he said with an accent. Maybe from Chicago. He extended his hand.

Charlie shook it. "Why Dutch?" she asked.

"Why not when I've been saddled with a name like Horatio?" he said, and Charlie and Aiden both laughed. "In school, all the kids wanted to make fun of it, but once I started working out and calling myself Dutch, nobody tried to kick my butt."

He had a formidable presence. Not the kind of guy you'd want to mess with unless you wanted a broken jaw.

"I can see why you brought him by," Charlie said to Aiden.

"It's not just for my sparkling personality," Dutch said.

Aiden tightened his arm around her. "Your start date has been bumped up. You're replacing Dutch on the Fugitive Apprehension Response Team day after tomorrow."

Charlie was taken aback. Part of her was eager to get back to work, but the other part enjoyed these languid evenings with Aiden, neither of them on call, neither in any danger. "Why so suddenly?"

"I leave tomorrow," Dutch said. "Special assignment undercover. I've read the file on the high-priority asset, but I have some questions that the file can't answer. I was hoping you two could."

"What does that have to do with us?" Charlie asked.

"It's regarding the data breach in San Diego," Dutch said. "We think we've found a way to possibly recover the Department of Justice hard drive that was stolen and prevent the sale of any more sensitive information. They want me to get close to the niece of the Los Chacales cartel leader. But I'll be working for your old boss, Will Draper. What can you tell me about him?"

Charlie rolled her eyes and blew out a harsh breath. "Nothing good. The only person Draper cares about is Draper. Rely on your own judgment, not his."

Aiden nodded. "This conversation is best done over drinks."

Lots and lots of drinks. "And dinner. I'm not much of a cook," Charlie said, "but I'm an expert at ordering good takeout."

"Were you told why you have to rush off so quickly?" Aiden asked.

"They said this is high priority and time sensitive. Apparently, there's a concern that the new identities of all the witnesses and the personal information of the marshals and their families in your region are going to be auctioned off to the highest bidder."

A chill ran down Charlie's spine. They knew the fallout of the data breach would far exceed Edgar Plinski, who was now in jail for the murder of Irene Guillory.

But no one would've imagined such sensitive information being auctioned off.

"Let's go inside. If there's anything we can tell you that might help you do your job, we're happy to share it," Charlie said, ushering Dutch in ahead of them.

She wrapped her arm around Aiden's waist, loving the feel of his immediate response to bring her closer, hold her tighter.

Their union was new and scary, but nothing had ever been more right. When they were together, the past didn't matter, the future was theirs to make of it whatever they wanted, and she was grateful for the present.

For the love and trust and respect between them that kept growing every day.

To some people, happiness was having a white picket fence, the marriage license and kids.

To Charlie, it was knowing that Aiden would kill to protect her and she would do the same for him. Come hell or high water, they had each other's back, and she wouldn't have it any other way.

Aiden kissed her, quick and sweet, but burning with desire. His fingers combed into her hair, locking her to him. Her heart thumped harder, filling with unfathomable joy. She'd never felt more loved or accepted in her life.

Here, with Aiden, she was safe. She was home.

* * * * *

The wind whipped off the lake, its chilly tentacles snaking into his thin black jacket, which he gathered at the neck with one raw hand, stiff with the cold. His other hand dipped into his pocket, his fingers curling around the handle of the gun.

His eyes darted toward the dark, glassy water and the rowboat bobbing against the shore before he stepped onto the road…and behind his prey.

She hobbled ahead of him, her shoes crunching the gravel, her body tilted to one side as she gripped her heavy cargo, which swung back and forth, occasionally banging against her leg.

A baby. Nobody said nothing about a baby.

He took a few steps after her and the sound of his boots grinding into the gravel seemed to echo through the still night. He froze.

When her footsteps faltered, he veered back into the reeds and sand bordering the lake. He couldn't have her spotting him and running off. What would she do with the baby? She couldn't run carrying a car seat. He'd hauled one of those things before with his niece inside and it was no picnic, even though Mindy was just a little thing.

He crept on silent feet, covering three or four steps to her one until he was almost parallel with her. Close enough to hear her singing some Christmas lullaby. Close enough to hear that baby gurgle a response.

The chill in the air stung his nose and he wiped the back of his hand across it. He licked his chapped lips.

Nobody said nothing about a baby.

The girl stopped, her pretty voice dying out, the car seat swinging next to her, the toys hooked onto the handle swaying and clacking. She turned on the toes of her low-heeled boots and peered at the road behind her, the whites of her eyes visible in the dark.

But he wasn't on the road no more.

He stepped onto the gravel from the brush that had been concealing him. Her head jerked in his direction. Her mouth formed a surprised O, but her eyes knew.

When he leveled his weapon at her, she didn't even try to run. Her knees dipped as she placed the car seat on the ground next to her feet.

She huffed out a sigh that carried two words. "My baby."

He growled. "I ain't gonna hurt the baby."

Then he shot her through the chest.

Don't miss Rookie Instincts *by Carol Ericson,*
available November 2020 wherever
Harlequin Intrigue books and ebooks are sold.

Harlequin.com

Get 4 FREE REWARDS!

We'll send you 2 FREE Books plus 2 FREE Mystery Gifts.

Harlequin Intrigue books are action-packed stories that will keep you on the edge of your seat. Solve the crime and deliver justice at all costs.

FREE Value Over $20

YES! Please send me 2 FREE Harlequin Intrigue novels and my 2 FREE gifts (gifts are worth about $10 retail). After receiving them, if I don't wish to receive any more books, I can return the shipping statement marked "cancel." If I don't cancel, I will receive 6 brand-new novels every month and be billed just $4.99 each for the regular-print edition or $5.99 each for the larger-print edition in the U.S., or $5.74 each for the regular-print edition or $6.49 each for the larger-print edition in Canada. That's a savings of at least 12% off the cover price! It's quite a bargain! Shipping and handling is just 50¢ per book in the U.S. and $1.25 per book in Canada.* I understand that accepting the 2 free books and gifts places me under no obligation to buy anything. I can always return a shipment and cancel at any time. The free books and gifts are mine to keep no matter what I decide.

Choose one: ☐ **Harlequin Intrigue**
Regular-Print
(182/382 HDN GNXC)

☐ **Harlequin Intrigue**
Larger-Print
(199/399 HDN GNXC)

Name (please print)

Address _____ Apt. #

City _____ State/Province _____ Zip/Postal Code

Email: Please check this box ☐ if you would like to receive newsletters and promotional emails from Harlequin Enterprises ULC and its affiliates. You can unsubscribe anytime.

Mail to the Reader Service:
IN U.S.A.: P.O. Box 1341, Buffalo, NY 14240-8531
IN CANADA: P.O. Box 603, Fort Erie, Ontario L2A 5X3

Want to try 2 free books from another series! Call 1-800-873-8635 or visit www.ReaderService.com.

Love Harlequin romance?

DISCOVER.

Be the first to find out about promotions, news and exclusive content!

Facebook.com/HarlequinBooks

Twitter.com/HarlequinBooks

Instagram.com/HarlequinBooks

Pinterest.com/HarlequinBooks

ReaderService.com

EXPLORE.

Sign up for the Harlequin e-newsletter and download a free book from any series at **TryHarlequin.com**

CONNECT.

Join our Harlequin community to share your thoughts and connect with other romance readers!
Facebook.com/groups/HarlequinConnection